TOM O'VIETNAM

BARON WORMSER

n
RIVERS
e
PRESS
W
MSUM

©2017 by Baron Wormser
First Edition
Library of Congress Control Number: 2016960045
ISBN: 978-0-89823-364-3
Ebook ISBN: 978-0-89823-365-0

Cover and interior design by Kendal Christenson
Author photo by Janet Wormser

The publication of *Tom o' Vietnam* is made possible by the generous support of
Minnesota State University Moorhead, the Dawson Family Endowment, and other
contributors to New Rivers Press.

For copyright permission, please contact Frederick T. Courtwright at
570-839-7477 or permdude@eclipse.net.

New Rivers Press is a nonprofit literary press associated with
Minnesota State University Moorhead.

Nayt Rundquist, Managing Editor
Kevin Carollo, Editor, MVP Poetry Coordinator
Travis Dolence, Director
George McCormack, MVP Prose Coordinator
Thomas Anstadt, Co-Art Director
Trista Conzemius, Co-Art Director
Thom Tammaro, Poetry Editor
Alan Davis, Editor Emeritus

Publishing Interns:
Laura Grimm, Anna Landsverk, Mikaila Norman

Tom o' Vietnam book team:
Taylor Brown, Kyle Courteau, Robyn Rohde

 Printed in the USA on acid-free, archival-grade paper.

 New Rivers Press
c/o MSUM
1104 7th Ave S
Moorhead, MN 56563
www.newriverspress.com

"The good years shall devour them, flesh and fell,
   Ere they shall make us weep: we'll see 'em starved first."

King Lear, William Shakespeare

"Life had made him old, he'd live it out old."

Dispatches, Michael Herr

"If America's soul becomes totally poisoned,
   part of the autopsy must read: Vietnam."

Martin Luther King, Jr.,
Riverside Church Speech,
April 4, 1967

FREEDOM IS
RELINQUISH
RELINQUISH
FREEDOM IS

*for those who served
and those who marched*

Endless swearing, a hoarse, braying wind of words, a weary, scornful, bemused reply to a war, swearing at those who were there and those who were not, at the army and the enemy, at death and life: everything blasted, withered, and coated by the tongue of injury. The question behind each insult and mockery being: What in the vast scheme of motley doings conspired to put me here? How did speeches spoken by gasbags of every stripe over decades come to endanger my modest network of blood? And if I wanted to be here, in my arrogance, manhood, confusion, enthusiasm, stupidity, patriotism, I must swear all the more. Who could have known?

Out, dunghill!

Swearing about food, rain, heat, women, officers, and, most of all, each other, each of us in the same unpredictable predicament. Swears coupled with other swears, vicious adjectives meeting nasty nouns: motherfucking shithead, goddamn asshole. Semi-swears, the ritual male abusing of male anatomy: you worthless little prick, the voice measured—a judgment—or light-hearted, oh, by the way. Long strings of swears blurring into one run-on, guttural frenzy. Or sometimes a simple "look, bitch," which starts a few shoves, shoulder pushes, and glares, the saying that you are a woman—a low blow. Swears for what seems like no reason, your voice mysteriously alive, proclaiming you are here in this faraway hell where, even on a good, un-murderous day, you are pissed. A reason can be found, if you want to go looking, but a lot of grim bile is in us already. Though not always bilious, everyone was once an infant gurgling, burping, unaffected by the droppings of time, though I think of guys like Briggs or Stone, who probably by the age of two were waiting to get bigger so they could get to Vietnam and start shooting people. Someone kicked them down the stairs early, the war on the home front. Or without the proclamation of reason or motive, like the tattoos: born to be bad, born to lose, born a conniving, chip-on-the-shoulder bastard.

Bastardy base? Base?

Briggs bought it, to use the lexicon you adopt when you see much random death. There wasn't a lot of him left either. He was what they call "remains." That doesn't matter, does it? Whether there's 98 percent of you intact or 32 percent. No open casket for him, if you like an open casket, and a lot of people do, death looking sort of rosy and peaceful, a time-out after the end of time. It's hard to make up for the missing 68 percent, though you never want to underestimate modern technology.

I remember a lot of deaths, some miscellaneous, some not. Some I heard about second- and third- and fourth-hand as facts became legends but they still got inside me.

Did you hear? Dost thou know me?

I was raised not to swear. It wasn't so much a sin because no one in my house cared about sin, we being take-it-easy-on-the-brimstone Protestants, social Christians who wake up on Christmas morning, remember Jesus, and then go back to sleep. It was because it was distasteful and bad manners. I agree with that. Swearing makes for a rotten take on life—ferocious, low-down, quick to find fault, the sum of your precious days little more than exasperation.

It worked, though, for the misery we were enduring. I bet even those serious, sweet-faced guys you see in Matthew Brady's photographs swore their churchgoing heads off. There should be a column of swears in the history books beside this or that war. Probably even Achilles and Hector bad-mouthed the other guys. Or maybe they were polite. Maybe they were real heroes and respected the men they were killing. I doubt it but maybe. Didn't Achilles drag Hector's body around at the back of a chariot? *Atrocity*—way more than a word—like what got done to some of our guys: mutilated real bad, their dicks cut off and stuffed in their mouths, and like we did to some of their guys. Anger that went past anger, way past.

See thyself, devil.

At first, before I went over there, when I was in basic and it was fuck-this and fuck-that, the swearing startled me. Do we have to curse everything? Must words be bullets? And even when I was there, I remember I told Stone one day when we were sitting around doing nothing that it was gratuitous. I talked like that—two years and two months of college, full of the mild eloquence of an English major's education. But what vocabulary was right? There was none, probably never has been, the government's language worse than swearing. Vietnamization—there's a word for you. There's a word to die for.

When I said that to Stone about "gratuitous" he looked at me like I just dropped a turd in his soup. Look, you educated faggot bitch, he said. He paused to smirk then laid what he considered wisdom on me: well, Tom boy, we'll see if your smart ass stays alive. Guys with too many words in their heads come out on the short side here.

How comes that?

You had that staying-alive thought in the back of your head and the front, too. You tried to push it away but it never left. I wondered sometimes if there were people who expected me to die, who were thinking, "Tom, he won't come back." You know, people in my hometown, going about their business, taking out a can of creamed corn from a grocery sack or closing the garage door and thinking, "Poor Tom." Or "Better him than me"—the perennial boundary of empathy. Or thinking nothing at all: "Tom, he gone."

I should have gotten the shivers from Stone because he was laying a curse on me but I was shivering all the time anyway. Standing upright and shivering, lying down and shivering, leaning over my food and shivering.

How dost, my boy? Art cold?

Bad night on the heath, Lear. Incoming torment.

When we were doing nothing and going nowhere, the guys would ask me, "Hey, College, tell us a story." I told them about Lear. How would you like it if you had two daughters who take what you give them—a lot of land and a big house—and then they treat you like squat? How would you like that? Once or twice, I extended the situation as in you could have nation problems. You're a big nation who goes to help some little nation that's getting pushed around but maybe it's not as simple as "getting pushed around." There's a civil war. There's a small mountain of barbed history. There's some thoughts called "ideology."

Ideo-what? What you say? Speak American.

He let his daughters fuck with him? Dude deserved it. Man's gotta be a man.

Thy element's below. Where is this daughter?

Like in a play, we talked back. No script beyond what we were making up but we talked back. It meant we were still alive. The storm hadn't come for us yet. We had no shelter, no hovel, but the storm that waited for each of us hadn't come yet.

It's the body that the swearing targets. Hard to be in a body, most of the time it works okay but it's permeable, easily invaded by foreign objects, fragmentary devices. And it's sad how the mind is always ridiculing the body, how its sexual organs are a source of contempt, and how The Act is always seen as obscene. Obscene? The dream of it was the oxygen we breathed.

Let copulation thrive. Let soldiers forget.
Let day relieve night.

I should ask the lieutenant. What happened?

I already told you back then.

No, I would say. You have to tell me again.

Soldier. (He would call me soldier. No matter how much time
went by, he would call me soldier, like a couple of decades after
Agincourt or Gettysburg or the Somme, and we meet in some bar
and we're still soldiers.) Soldier, we engaged the enemy. As you know,
we took some casualties. According to our body count (he would
pause there because he liked to savor any official type language) we
killed seven of them. Some VC, some sympathizers.

"CC" we called the lieutenant, the Corpse Counter. Did they do
that when Napoleon fought battles? Walk around afterward and
count the dead? The VC took their dead with them anyway. The
people who got killed weren't enemy. They were people who were
trying to stay alive. They were people living in their godforsaken
village that was a happy village once upon a time with children running around barefoot and pigs rooting and old ladies gossiping and
everyone praying to whatever gods floated their boat.

Don't bring God into it, soldier.

Things with the lieutenant would go downhill from there. If I've
gotten into the house in a suburb somewhere in Texas, and if the
little lady is home, she'll ask me if I want an iced tea and I'll say Yes,
ma'am. The lieutenant will make a strained face like he's got to make
a bowel movement and ask how it's going, despite his knowing how
it's going, and not just for me. Every day one of us makes it onto the
front page: shoots himself, shoots his old lady, shoots some buddy
of his, gets shot by some buddy of his. Some of us haven't adapted
well. Hard to get rid of the reek of war inside of us.

Who gives anything to poor Tom?

I'll tell him I've been reading *King Lear* again, that actually I never
stop reading it; that it's like a bible to me.

That's by Shakespeare, isn't it? His wife says that when she brings in the iced tea on a tray. She smiles but it's a serious smile. Shakespeare is someone who counts. No matter the bleak, conjured reality, he's an important notion.

You get lost in the library, Tom? asked Knightley.

I look at the iced tea on the tray and the lieutenant's appropriate wife who looks nice in her J.C. Penney dress and I want to start bawling. I lack the simplest things, like a woman who gets her hair done every two weeks bringing iced tea on a metal tray that's decorated with some flowers to suggest a modest notion of beauty. I think the flowers are supposed to be pansies. I think of Doreen. She likes flowers. Are those pansies on that tray, ma'am?

The lieutenant could feel at that point that things might be starting to get out of hand. He might say again, if he was in the right mood, not a good mood but a responsible mood—his idea of empathy—that I did what I had to do, that I was a soldier. Duty, he'd say. It was a big small word but we all had heard it, though really we were just some young bodies with heads on them talking about getting laid and drinking beer and our girls back home–how some of them kiss a photo of us each night and some are cunts getting spooned while our insides get turned outside. And our cars. Don't forget the cars.

To leave so soon, your speech not yet begun.

How do you like your tea?

Half a teaspoon of sugar, please.

Hot out there today.

Hot? Try steamy jungle hot. Try vegetable hell. Try the earth on steroids where stuff can't stop growing, like it's talking to you day and night because it can't stop growing. And you can't stop listening. You're sitting or lying down or you're walking and you hear the jungle and it's not like anything you know because you grew up in the temperate zone where there's winter and spring. Your skin itches and you think you can hear stuff growing, a sound like beetles chewing wood, faint but steady.

Want to know what we are? Fertilizer, said Knightley.

More tea?

Take heed o' th' foul fiend.

The lieutenant wants me gone. I can't blame him. This vet stuff gets tiresome. I want myself gone but lack the willpower. Or I like sitting in this living room and thinking this could have been my life, with beige curtains and matching French-something furniture and a chandelier in the foyer, tasteful, not too sparkly. I didn't have to take everything personally. It was only a war.

When I get up to leave, the lieutenant and his wife trade glances: he's going to leave. Did they think I would stay forever? They can diddle from one day to another and be Americans and talk about what's new and exciting. I'm the one who's stuck in *forever*.

I figure Lear doesn't live long after Cordelia dies.

You got it. Man dies right on the spot. Right there in front of everybody.

Seven bodies are what the lieutenant counted. Math whiz. Does a young girl count for half a body?

Thanks for your hospitality. Thanks for telling me I have nothing to absolve, though I doubt if that word is in the lieutenant's vocabulary. Maybe you don't even hear it in church these days. I wouldn't know. I tried that window but it wouldn't open.

You did what you did, soldier.

That's tautological but true. We were taking fire and I turned around and saw someone starting to throw something and I shot. How old was she? You counted the bodies. How old was she?

Guys said you could tell how old the bodies were from their teeth, except they didn't go to dentists the way we did so it was tricky. You can measure the quality of life according to how many dentists there are.

Thanks for the tea.

I make it myself.

7

Take care of yourself, soldier. You aren't guilty of anything.

I'm ashamed, though. I'm ashamed.

Neither of them says come again. They shut the oversize wooden front door, which looks like giants live there not people. I walk a few steps but stop. I'm a little shaky. I don't want to be but I'm a little shaky. It's like my bones want to leave my flesh. It's good they're not looking at me because I took a bus and then walked a couple miles. All that talking about Fords and Chevs like it was God and The Devil. I bought a car when I got back but sold it. Buses improve your social life.

Maybe I'll stand on the sidewalk for awhile. No more social calls to pay today. I've forfeited my purposes.

Their azaleas look a little wilted. Texas does that.

Everyone was screaming. There was so much noise and everyone was screaming. I was screaming, too.

She had something in her hand. She was going to throw it.

Last month Ramos had bought it.

Some kid threw a grenade, one of ours.

Ramos played the harmonica. Knightley said it was mournful music, music to make you cry over your mother's grave. Ramos put down his harmonica and made a goofy smile. Then he played some more.

They're little people. It's hard to tell who's a kid. They don't live on hamburgers and milk shakes like us.

On the playground, all the kids are running, loping, skipping, jumping. I used to do that, too. Every second was so full. Like being an animal. Shouting for the sake of shouting. Being free.

Do, de, de, de. Sessa!

What she had in her hand was a doll made of some balled up cloth with these pearly buttons for eyes. She had drawn a smile on the face. The hair was some kind of animal hair, maybe from one of those buffaloes they had there. It was fine, though, not coarse.

Everything happened fast. When someone fell down on the playground, everyone ran over fast to see what happened. I can hear the teacher blow her whistle. It meant we were supposed to stop having fun and make a line to go back in. Not everybody stopped. I usually stopped, though, because even when I was a kid, I was like that; someone who listened to what people told him to do. Must have been why I wound up in the Army. Later, you muttered about what you were told to do, but you did it.

Did I see the doll? Did I go to the other side of the world to see a girl holding a doll?

Could be, Knightley would say. He was full of philosophical expertise, like he knew something the rest of us didn't know, like being a Negro gave him extrasensory perception. Maybe it did. He got on some guys' nerves but not mine. I liked him. I told him once, back here, about how at random moments I see the doll floating above my head, sort of serene with that drawn-on smile. Then it blows up.

Tom, he said, that's a hallucination. You been smoking too much weed?

I used to but I gave it up. I've got too much grief to carry around habits too.

Ask poor Tom. He'll tell you.

World, world, O world!

There always would be some girls on the playground with their dolls. They'd form a little circle and they'd talk to their dolls and comb their hair and sometimes swap clothes from one doll to another. I know because my sisters used to bring their dolls to school sometimes. I can still see how serious their faces were when they were playing. It wasn't really playing. It was practice for being moms, for caring.

The guys were running around yelling and pointing their fingers at each other and going bam you're dead. Guys were falling down who knew they'd been shot or wounded. Sometimes they'd say you only grazed me and pop back up.

The girls were cooing to their dolls. The teacher was strolling around thinking some adult thought. She might as well have been the president.

How far my eyes may pierce I cannot tell.

And I can't tell but I have an idea. That's one of my problems. I've always got an idea, like Lear, a head full of ideas. He's a hard man but I've grown to like him. He's so confused, so confident, and then it all falls apart and I'm there railing at him in a good-natured but desperate way. And he's taking it. He's listening, which is more than most guys I knew ever did. Sure, guys would say. Sure. Meaning I've already got enough shit on my plate, buddy. And they did. But Lear starts listening. Not that it does him any good. Maybe it makes him even crazier. Before, he was just imagining. Then he starts to realize it's worse than imagining, it's real. It's a place where you can't take anything back.

Like war?

Like war.

Sometimes I ask my nieces, who would be Amy's kids since Evie has boys and Paula doesn't have kids, about their dolls. They wrinkle their little noses. What's a man doing asking about dolls? Doesn't he get it? I tell them I like dolls. They still look at me funny, like mom's brother is crazy as everyone says he is, but he buys us stuff when he has money and he never gets angry at us. He always tells us how good we are.

He cries a lot, though. He'll be in his little room upstairs and you can hear him crying.

I don't think that Lear cries. That's part of his problem—the not crying. The crying is part of the problem, but that's different. If Lear could have cried, he wouldn't have been Lear. He'd have been some therapeutic relic sitting in a VA hospital upchucking his emotional innards and getting nothing back for it beyond a few nods and a doc's surreptitious glance at his wristwatch. Lunch time coming? Maybe he's having an affair with one of the nurses and they've got an hour at the motel down the highway. Maybe he's bored and hungry.

Stay positive, someone will say. Stay positive, Tom, which makes me feel like I'm some scientific molecule. No one in Lear's world would say that. Science and technology haven't gotten between people and life yet. Everything that comes out of their mouths is so physical that you can imagine it rotting back into the earth. They're all lumpy and sticky, darkness and shadows, kind of like the guys in the jungle, spitting, grunting, fuck-this and fuck-that.

Fellows, hold the chair.
Upon these eyes of thine I'll set my foot.

Fuck death. Lear would have said that at the end but he couldn't. Eloquence betrayed him.

The girls are cooing over their dolls and sometimes a guy will stop and look at the girls and wonder what that's all about. Is that love? Is that just something girls do? Should he ask them? It's just a second. Anything longer than that will be like going AWOL from being a guy. None of that jive, brother. Get on your horse and ride. Every other guy's pointing a finger at you.

How far my eyes may pierce I cannot tell.

I lie on a bed and see to the other side of the world. It's daytime and the village is still there. A little girl is playing with a doll. She's very careful because this doll is made of some sticks and could fall apart real easy. She's very careful because it could blow up. She understands that.

My folks had three girls in a row and then they had me. Then they called it quits. The word I heard was that my dad was waiting for a boy. Primogeniture, divvying up the kingdom, the once and future prince—Tom o' Nowhere.

Over the years since my return to American civilization, I move around the woman circuit—sisters, mother, on-and-off lovers. They listen to me, give me advice that I don't follow, and fuss over me until they get politely sick of me, which is when I buy a bus ticket. Cozy rooms in the back of the house or in the attic with spare beds, calm as graves. I make the bed, no need for maid service. Neatness soothes me. If nothing means anything, if you can be talking and then step on a claymore and be gone just like that, your voice still in the air and the smell of you and your boot's imprint in the earth, there's a lot to be said for tucking in sheets, for getting them nice and precise. The sheets aren't masquerading as something else. I like to run a hand over them for reassurance.

There's Tom up in his room touching the sheets. He takes a half-hour to make his bed. No one complains about a neatly made bed, though.

The fit is on me.

> I visited hell
> Lost my head, heart and face.
> It's okay, though,
> I gained a lot of inner space.

Lear didn't consider the fool to be a person, not that he was any good at considering anyone to be a person. If you're a king, it might cancel out that kind of considering. Or you never do that kind of considering in the first place. Or you pretend, the way someone like Henry Kissinger pretends, that other people matter when he knows they don't because they aren't him.

Who the fuck is that? Knightley asked. I was looking at a picture of Kissinger and Knightley was looking over my shoulder. Some important motherfucker, I bet. Ugly, even for a white dude. Got those elephant ears.

Too bad he couldn't be introduced like that. Here he is—Some Important Motherfucker. Let's give him some incoming rounds of applause. Fighting a war does take the pretense out of you, not that I had much to begin with. I've never liked mirrors or buying clothes. When I was a kid I liked to pretend I was an animal. Goat, tiger,

camel—you name it. I'd loon around in the backyard, galumph-
ing, trotting, leaping. My sisters would smile—Something Boys Did.
Sometimes I'd make up a companion. I'd be out there jabbering to
the air. The great thing was that the air would talk back. I could be
two people.

My face I'll grime with filth, Blanket my loins, elf all my hairs
in knots.

That's not something in the human ballpark, that's a diseased
imagination, that's a kind of lost that never gets found.

Shoot it. I'm telling you, shoot it.

As I say, I can spend a long time making the bed. I can rumple
the sheets pretty bad—the nightmare does that and then tossing and
wondering why I'm bothering to live a life. Sometimes, though, I
don't have to touch the bed because I've slept on the floor. No one
can see in or shoot me down there. I slept on the ground plenty. You
get used to it. It's where you came from and where you're headed.

What makes the nightmare especially awful is that it's silent. I'm
shooting and everyone's shooting but it's silent. It happens a little
slower than in life and there are gaps where I don't know where I am.
But then I do. I want the silence to be over but there's no piercing it.
It's like a shroud over everything. It's all wrong and I know it's wrong
but there's nothing I can do. And it's in me, a lot of bad silence.

Let me have surgeons; I am cut to th' brains.

One of the good things about America, right up there with baseball and Jimi Hendrix, is the library. You can sit all day and read and
no one bothers you. Maybe what I was fighting for was the library.
It's the home for words but not like "We're here to stop communism." Those were words that just floated around and that people
said over and over but they didn't mean anything. They were like
saying "Bless you" when someone sneezed, automatic. They were
crazy words, but I doubt if anyone ever got up at a press conference
and asked the president or the secretary of defense or some sena-
tor what exactly "stop" meant. Stop? We stopped some bullets that

came from words. Stop? Like you put your hand up at a crosswalk when the children were going to school and you stopped the traffic, like America was some kind of crossing guard. Stop?

May not an ass know when the cart draws the horse?

Words are nets. We get tangled the way Lear gets tangled, the way he loses it when Cordelia says, "Nothing." She's telling it like it is but he can't take it. He wants words to be like the stuffing in a couch or packaging material or like the army where you get an order and say "Yessir" and that's it, there's nothing more to think about. The words fill a space and you can nod your head like everything's okay because the space got filled. Lear's a king and a king is an army guy. People do what he tells them to do. He's not used to thinking twice. Why should he? So when Cordelia tells him "Nothing," it's like a pit opens up beneath him but he doesn't even know what a pit is. He's never fallen because of words. He's just acted and acted and acted.

Over there, I saw a couple guys get Dear John letters. They'd bluff their way through and maybe swear at the bitch who had "to move on" or "this is too hard, I'm lonely," which maybe it was or maybe some other dude was fucking her better than you ever did but what happened first for the guy holding that piece of paper was this dull look into space, this what-the-hell look. That was the pit. It opened up and the guy fell like Lear fell. Lear keeps falling through the whole play, falling and falling. No bottom to it. Cordelia's death isn't even the end of it because he's still there holding her body. Anguish goes on like outer space. There's no end to it.

You gonna pick her up? Tom, you gonna pick her up? She's dead. Get a fucking grip.

I touched a body but it wasn't a body like you think of a body. It was more missing than here. It was soft. I went to move it but it wasn't there to be moved. It was squishy or like jelly, like it had no bones. I didn't know what to do. I pulled my hand back. It was hard to believe there was going to be more time after something like that.

Welcome then,
Thou unsubstantial air that I embrace.

In the library, mornings are best. There's restfulness, everything peaceful after the night, even the dust feels fresh, every calm mote in its place. People slowly pull out their wooden chairs at the reading tables. The outdoors sifts in through tall windows. If it's winter, the radiators are going, gasping little warm sighs. It's so gentle that I could sit and read the newspaper, gather some events—a battle in another war somewhere, a speech, a Supreme Court ruling—shake my head, wrinkle my forehead, or just keep turning the pages, concerned and serious. There's Tom, a regular citizen, doing his civic duty, keeping current, a believer in the ways of the known world.

Once you are a part of the 5,000-more-GIs-news—the rational madness—and then you're not even that and you understand that all there is going to be is more news; a waterfall that doesn't stop, that has an idle, malicious life of its own. Then you give up on the news because the news that I came to—Tom's news, a grunt's news, the news from a woman cleaning the headquarters' floors at one a.m., the child running down the path from her village and clutching her doll, the bar girl asking "You go boom-boom?"—that news will never be there.

I speak the noise of the crazed air. I speak the jets smoking the sky. I speak the gun of every mouth.

What hast thou been?

Good gentlemen, go your gait and let poor voke pass.

He means "folk." He has an accent.

I like to stop somewhere on the way to the library, some local scene, Wally's or Mary's, where the waitresses don't wear corporate uniforms. I have a cup of coffee and watch people around me who are busier than I am, which is pretty much everybody. I dropped out. Or I was dropped out, though not like guys we dropped out of helicopters.

I met a guy who helped push a captured VC out of a helicopter. He said that "a body fell pretty fast." That's what he said, thoughtful like he was talking about a high school physics experiment. "He was a zero," he said. "You can't subtract zero." A lot of what happened when it became talk was like that—no big thing, explanations and embroideries that kept everyone going and acting as though they were sane, which maybe is like any day on earth, milder of course, but still the same. Some people in a castle, some people out in a storm, someone sitting in a hovel poking at a fire, everyone numb but making sentences.

The guy who told me that was an interrogator. That's what Lear does to Cordelia. He's trying to break her down because he can't accept what she has to say. I think people don't get how much of an army guy Lear is, how he wants all his buddies around who are also army guys so they can raise their own version of American Legion hell, pound down all the beers they want, whoop it up, and generally act like assholes. I don't blame Lear's daughters for not wanting that crowd around. Imagine if I showed up at any of my sisters' houses with a pack of guys I was in the war with. Some of the guys would be spooked, too, in that way the jungle spooked you, too much of everything breathing on you and touching you like something you were afraid of when you were a kid. Some of the guys could be unpredictable.

My mind runs away with me.

In the play you don't meet Lear's guys. Maybe Shakespeare understood that his audience would understand what these guys were like and he didn't have to fill up the stage with them. If I staged the play, I'd fill up the back of the stage with guys hoisting Budweisers and bragging and bullshitting to each other. His daughters could have handled things better but it makes you think. Why does he need those guys? It's because he's army and army is a pack.

I can spend a lot of time with that morning coffee. It's solace or it's more like it's supposed to be solace. I've got a lot of *supposed* going on with me. "Now make sure you have your cup of coffee,

Tom" one of my sisters will say to me like I'm so dumb I don't how to take care of myself, because to them I don't. I'm homeless, a wanderer on the heath, an exclaimer of serious nonsense, a man with no fixed domicile or occupation, though to me it's the opposite: I've got lots of homes. What do they say in the army? I rotate.

The coffee doesn't always work, though it seems to work for the people around me. They're busy. They're getting fueled up on some high-test. For me, coffee is more like a buddy who doesn't say anything smart or dumb. There's that space, though, between the coffee and me. Sometimes I can sit with that space and fill it up—hand to mouth, hand to mouth, hand to mouth. I'm a puppet running myself. Sometimes I find myself sitting there.

Can't do it. In the army, over and over you do it: shoot, lift, drill, march, listen, salute, eat, drink, stand, look, run, crawl. It's like the primers in elementary school. See the soldier. See the soldier run. See the soldier run fast. See the soldier yell. Go soldier.

It's like a dream.

You start dreaming, you get your ass killed.

Hoist that cup of Joe, kid. It doesn't weigh much. You can do it. Everyone else does it. If I start studying other people the coffee gets cold. I get lost. The tripwire gets tripped. I don't want that to happen, though more than one woman has told me I do want the tripwire to go off. It's always better to sound the alarm.

Bring some covering for this naked soul.

Why am I alive? Johnson, Briggs, Vernon. They're not. I've got some names. Want to hear their stories?

I don't. I want to drink a cup of coffee like these other vokes. I want to be with the other vokes. It's safe there. Maybe you spill some, that's about all the trouble you're in for. You apologize. You get some stain remover.

How you doing, darling? Little more? Top it off? Over easy? Wheat toast? Still brooding about that war you were in? You gotta let things go, honey.

Let me explain myself. I am a man who came from unnatural dealing rendered natural, my tenuous life numbered, drafted, and processed, ready to be mutilated.

What words are these?

Stain remover, I need to remember to tell that to the next shrink. They like it when you're metaphorical and something like funny. It indicates you're getting something like better, getting some perspective, not sitting in a coffee shop and crying into your fucking coffee with people staring at you and you can't stop and you stumble out of the place trying to act cool, like I do this every morning: cry into my coffee, it's no big deal, just part of my routine. Have a good one. Don't step on a land mine. Don't swear unnecessarily either.

I first read *King Lear* in college—Intro to Lit. 101, not the world's most beguiling course description. The prof was a little bantam of a guy who strutted around, declaimed, and put some heavy eye contact on the young women in the room. Imagine getting to spend your life doing that. He knew stuff, though. He'd studied up. He showed us how one thing has to do with another, how Gloucester and Lear are two sides of the same confused coin and how every word is working, how the play is a big poem. That's probably not revelatory but it was to me. As I sat there in my little dorm room while my roommate—Rick from Racine—scratched his balls or asked me to loan him a dollar, I could feel that I was entering something that had nothing to do with me but did. It was like when another car ran into my car. I was starting to go through a green and the other car ran a red. I watched as the hood of my car crumpled and the whole car shuddered and screamed and my head went toward the windshield. There's that moment when you think your life is going to change forever—right now. There's that moment when you think that this isn't happening but it is.

It is.

That wasn't what we got asked on a test. I don't remember the test. I remember sitting in that room in that five-story dormitory with its green cinder block walls and fire exit signs and feeling weirdly comforted.

This is the worst. That's comforting to learn the worst, how dark the night can be. Or think you know the worst, you with your Led Zeppelin posters and your stereo and your books making a neat, upright row like soldiers. I'm safe. I will wake up in the morning.

> To be worst,
> The lowest and most dejected thing of fortune,
> Stands still in esperance, lives not in fear.

I carried a paperback around in the war until there was nothing much left of it. Tom's Book, the guys called it. Whenever we moved around, Knightley would tell me, "Now don't forget your book." One more charm to ward off dread—rabbit's feet, dice, St. Christopher medals. A guy named Amundsen carried a photo of his wife's snatch.

Esperance means hope.

Nice sound to it. Like a chick's name.

How come Lear's wife's not in the play? After awhile, the platoon guys started asking me questions like our discussion group back in college every Tuesday afternoon where the teaching assistant listened to our arguments and opinions.

Tom, you coming down for breakfast? You going to the library today? You have an appointment?

Those three daughters didn't just pop out of the toaster. What was she doing while Lear was rollicking with his buddies? He was her master but she must have gotten the better of him in those ways that women out-maneuver men, the first one being that they let men think they know something. I learned that from watching three sisters. Cordelia, though, was stubborn like her father. Her mother could have told her to take it easy, but then her mother might already have flamed out or been smothered by her over-and-over duties or died in childbirth. A lot of women died giving birth. There's no remarkable play about them. They were just gone the way that Lear's wife is gone, the way that everything that dies is gone and how you're supposed to be good with that. Maybe Lear was still grieving for his wife. Maybe when Cordelia protested her love it brought the pain back.

I know from corresponding with Professor Cohen, who's a Shakespeare scholar but not the little bantam who taught me, that my speculations are silly. It's a play. They aren't real people. He's gentle with me because I'm a 'Nam guy and mayhem may be my middle name but he tells me that you have to proceed with what's on the page. And I agree, but only up to a point. It seems to me that if you can't imagine the people as real people, it's all sort of stupid, some sort of exercise you do that's more out of life than in life. "I'm not sure about that," the professor will write me about some speculation. I'm not sure either, believe me.

Something he left imperfect in the state.

Behind my speculations are my senses which I trust. I've got a good nose, keen hearing. In the coffee shops or on the buses, they're busy, Sniff and Listen, part of the Here We Are Team. And I'm appreciative. Even at the buses' stale, airless worst, which can get pretty unpleasant like dirty laundry you left under a bed, it doesn't bug me. It's human: spilled milk, spilled Coca-Cola, fried chicken, hard boiled eggs, spearmint gum, cigarettes, farts, body odor, cheap perfume, cheap cologne, hair tonic, Dentyne, Listerine, french fries. None of it is as funky as guys in the jungle who haven't seen a shower for days, who itch like crazy, whose skin feels like you could peel it off. We seriously stank.

On account of the smells, dogs would really enjoy buses but they don't let them on unless someone's blind and it's a seeing-eye dog. Those dogs are usually Shepherds like the dogs we had in Vietnam. I met a couple of dogs over there I really liked, particularly the dog Bandit. Bandit could smell the enemy. The army trained him to smell the clothes of the enemy. He was smarter that way than any of us soldiers. And he could get nasty if he had to because he wanted to protect us. He knew we were at war.

I heard that the army killed all the dogs, the ones that didn't got shot in combat, because they couldn't go back to America where there was no war. They were unfit for peacetime. Do I grasp the irony in this? Even if he doesn't know the word, irony is one of the basic courses a soldier studies. When you think about that, Lear wasn't much of a soldier—no irony in him. Or he was like a major. They don't have any irony in them either.

5,000 more GIs.

I have no way, and therefore want no eyes.

I've traveled through Central America. People there bring everything onto buses: chickens, dogs, pigs, goats. I remember sitting beside a goat. It's hard to know what a goat's thinking. It looks like they're thinking, they can get a pretty serious face on them, but maybe they aren't. Maybe they're just busy being a goat and that's it.

How does Tom spend his time? Thinking about goats thinking.

Life in the States would be better if they let animals on buses. They might shit here and there but it wouldn't be much worse than the smells I told you about. The fact is I don't remember any animals shitting on any bus I was on down there. We worry about making a mess. We mess up some country on the other side of the world but we won't allow some chicken, that's in a cage anyway, to make a mess on a bus.

Don't go there, Tom. That's what my sister Evie says. Don't go there, Tom.

And where am I going? I say to her.

You're going to the critical place, the unhappy place. Dissatisfaction City, America's Most Un-American Town.

But I heard myself proclaimed. Do you understand? It means I am in serious trouble, on the most wanted posters. Tom o' Vietnam Wanted for Unruly Thinking, Quoting Shakespeare in Public Places, Making Bad Decisions in Wartime, and Being Born.

I like to walk or take a local bus to the Greyhound station and see where I might go. I like to notice whatever's going on around me. I've

21

thought of becoming a bird watcher because I used to think about what was happening to the birds and animals while hell was being unleashed. Did anyone ask their permission? We translate everything into us, the human mob, but the view from our heads tends to be narrow.

Don't go there.

Evie lives in Santa Fe where she runs an art gallery. It's not great stuff she's selling; more like stuff people buy to fill a space on a too-big wall in their too-big house. She's been divorced twice, a kid from each marriage. Now she's married to the desert and mountains. And the light, she downright purrs about the light.

I've got some weight I need to move, I say to the man at the bus ticket counter. He gives me a raised eyebrow but I'm in earnest, so he is, too. Freight? He asks. In a sense, I say. And in what sense would that be? He asks, giving me the there's-one-like-this-every-day-or-so look. The flesh on my bones, I say.

I guess that's a way of putting it.

All the way to Chicago. I've got a sister who lives there.

Well, that's great. The Windy City. You want a ticket?

I'll see their trial first. Bring in their evidence. Look first to those rags that hide nothing.

Edgar—the origin of the Abominable Tom—lives through what he lives through. He has his choices. It's not like people don't kill themselves in Shakespeare. It happens all the time. They can't stand it anymore and do something about it. The space gets more and more narrow and then there is no space. Edgar, though, hides out in a tree where he becomes someone else. Was Tom always there inside of Edgar waiting to come out? Does everyone have a Tom inside himself or herself? I know it's a play and you're not supposed to ask questions like that. It shows you're artless and simple. Okay, I'm artless and simple. I still wonder. Shakespeare is supposed to make you wonder.

I should have asked the lieutenant. I wonder how many daughters in this village died. I wonder, overall, how many daughters died. That's not talking about rapes, just deaths.

The wonder is he hath endured so long.

Evie pours herself a glass of white wine after she comes home from the gallery and we talk. Mostly it's about when I'm going to sort my life out. She's a big sorter. Most women are. Maybe it's the hen instinct. I don't blame her, though, because sorting hasn't been my strong suit. When I got out of 'Nam, I thought, well, I'll go back to school. This will be easy. I'll pick up where I left off.

Where I left off was how I got kicked out of the university for violating rules—being in a girl's room when I wasn't supposed to be in a girl's room. They used to have rules like that and they used to enforce them, whether a war was going on or not. Another war was going on: The War against Sex. The sad thing was that I wasn't making any real time with this girl. Cindy was her name. I'd start to touch her and she'd back off. "Not now, Tom," she'd say. "Not now." I hadn't discovered the phrase "If not now, when" yet. Anyhow, the dorm mother knocked on the door and we'd lost track of time in our going nowhere with one another. The dorm mother, a hefty woman with a hefty bosom, waded in as if entering a crowded barroom and cleared her throat. I wasn't supposed to be there. Cindy had all her clothes on and I had mine on. We could have been talking about Shakespeare. Yes, I wasn't supposed to be there past nine o'clock. And, yes, the door was supposed to be ajar. "There will be consequences," she announced. And there were.

So you're here, Tom, because you got caught with some girl that you weren't even doing anything with? Do I have that right? Because if I do, you are a sadder son of a bitch than I thought you were, which is pretty damn sad.

I stood in some dean's office and he told me in a voice like he had to be somewhere else that there were rules and I'd broken them and was being asked to leave.

Asked? I asked.

That's a polite way of saying you are done here, he said. Good luck. He didn't extend a hand across his desk. You might have thought I'd shot someone.

My father laughed a harsh laugh. My mother cried. My best friend from high school told me I was a joke. My sisters were off leading their lives. I could have gone to Canada. I could have done something to myself to get deferred when draft morning came. I could have said I won't go. I could have done a bunch of things but I stayed around our house and got involved with a girl who was at loose ends the way I was and who let me do what we both needed to do.

When the letter came, I told my parents I was going to go. My father said he respected me. My mother went upstairs and closed the bedroom door. One of our neighbors stopped by to tell me he was a hawk and I was more of a man than he thought I was.

What are you, sir?

I am stuff, such as the moon is made of, the antipodes, the remotest Bermudas, the fluff of weeds that roams with the wind, the radio's electric chants.

War thing, you make my heart sing.

Don't start, Tom. Life isn't poetry. My second-in-line sister, Amy, would say that. What did she have against words? My third-in-line sister, Paula, told me that Amy's heart got broken in high school. She wanted to die, Paula said. Maybe Amy stayed in her bedroom and wrote poems. Maybe they only made it worse.

Evie asks when I'm leaving.

> I'll look no more
> Lest my brain turn,
> My mind catch fire
> My mute eyes burn.

Lear makes his own trouble. If a man makes his own trouble, he's gotta live with that trouble. You see it that way, Tom? None of us here made our own trouble. Someone made this trouble for us.

We inherited it. Now we're making more trouble but it's not like we got the trouble started. Your man Lear started the trouble.

Knightley went to college, too. Some black college in North Carolina. He got bored. He said it wasn't living.

So going to war is living?

Makes you feel alive when you could die any minute, doesn't it?

You're much deceived.

I ask Evie if she wants me to leave.

Do I mind having your dreamy, edgy ass around here? You play wiffle ball with the boys. You do the dishes. You make pretty good chili for someone who doesn't live in New Mexico. You barely drink, which is more than I can say for me. Evie looks downcast when she says that. But you want to have a life, don't you, something more than a spare room in your sister's not-very-well-kept-up hacienda with her two boys clamoring for a father?

I tell her I do have a life. When your life is in jeopardy, you appreciate getting up in the morning, even if you've been sleeping on the floor, maybe more because you've been sleeping on the floor. You're not looking for the Disney version. Walking down the street is fine.

Spare me the wisdom, she says. Randomly, though it's probably not random at all, you go up to your room and I hear you crying. I don't get that. I mean how you start crying, how it's like you have to leave the room because you're sick and then you disappear. I think it's what in the news they call "trauma." It's not whimpering. It's crying. Men don't cry like that, like they're going to pieces.

Maybe they should.

What's in a word? A lost depth calls to me.

Evie looks thoughtful. I could have used a few tears from the two I was with. One was Teflon plated, the other was cast iron. When I cried—and I cried plenty—they looked at me like I just wandered in from another planet. The Planet of Female Emotion. Or they stroked my hair and told me it would be okay, things will get better, babe, some bullshit line when they had no sense of what

I was crying about because it wasn't real to them. It was just something that women did, like bleed every month.

Something's broken in me. I'm trying to fix it but it's broken.

Something's broken in everyone, Tom. The world wouldn't be this way, if something weren't broken in everyone. There wouldn't be these goddamn wars for starters. And the speeches that are almost worse than the wars. I'm waiting for someone to stand up and say, look I don't know what I'm doing. Can you help me?

I've got her going. I didn't mean to.

That's not going to happen. That would be like Teflon or cast iron saying I don't know, without any babe or sugar at the end, just I don't know. Those may be the strangest words of all.

Canst tell why one's nose stands in the middle of one's face?

I make a funny face, move the tip of my nose with my index finger. Evie smiles a little. It's not like I don't hear her. She's my sister. She saw me at the airport the day I came back. She looked at me and she started crying. I couldn't cry back then. I knew how to shiver but I couldn't cry. She hugged me hard, as hard as my mom hugged me.

I know that one, Tom, she says. The boys like your riddles.

Among the things Shakespeare understood is the importance of fools. No one's asking me but I don't think it's the political system that needs to change. It's not about a better ism. There isn't any. It's that there needs to be fools beside every king and president and prime minister, fools who are allowed their foolery. The fools should have their sly say, their equal time. Every balloon wants a pin.

The reason why the seven stars are no more than seven is a pretty reason.

Because they are not eight.

Evie and I are quiet for a while, then we go out to look at the night sky. It's cold but although I've only got a tee shirt on, I like it. When I'm in the desert, the stars always seem even more distant. The big religions came from the desert. You can feel alone in the desert in a way that's different from other aloneness. God came from that aloneness.

Keep me in temper oh you kind gods.

We still don't say anything. She's my biggest sister, as she likes to say. She's been studying me forever. I can wait for her to talk. The stars are in no hurry. I feel free of myself.

You ever hear from that girl, the one you were in the room with? Did they kick her out, too? I forget.

They kicked her out. She said she hated me. She said I ruined her life. You don't hear from people who feel you ruined their life.

We're both taking in the stars, heads up, talking more to them than to one another.

It was all so stupid. I can feel Evie shaking her head in the moonless night. One gift of the war: you can feel things in the dark.

Do the stars, Evie, do they feel especially distant to you here?

No, they seem closer, neighborly. The desert changes your sense of what's near and what's far.

You didn't have to go, Tom. That's what I don't understand. There were ways out. It's not like you believed in that war.

I think we've talked about this before, sister. It's been some years. Let's stay with the stars. Otherwise, I could start to wobble.

She comes over to me, puts a hand on my shoulder. She's one of those women who can't wear enough jewelry, silver rings and bracelets. You know what?

What?

I'm happy I'm not a man.

I expect to start wobbling but I'm solid inside, not a happy solid, but solid, dense with grief that has its own weight.

She leaves her hand on me. It's a precious weight.

My itinerary, dear sister: I'm going to see our sister Amy. And I'm going to see this professor I've been writing to. I want to meet him. He wants to meet me.

Evie turns me around and puts her face up close to mine. You don't have to do everybody's work, Tom. You could just do your own.

27

I wouldn't be Tom then, but I don't say that. I say that I hear her because I do.

The night goes on being the night; the stars go on being the stars. We're in such a big, long picture.

Saying goodbye to her boys is hard. Who is this guy who comes and goes? We stand in the kitchen before they head off to school and make a circle. We start to bay like dogs together. We get into it, dipping our heads and outdoing each other, making high sounds, low sounds, a whole little dog opera. When we're done—and it takes some minutes—we put our heads together and rub them against one another. Then we're really done. They're boys again. I'm whoever I am. They go out to wait for the school bus. We don't wave.

> My doggerel heart's
> About to explode.
> This veteran's splitting
> For the open road.

Evie watches this while bustling around the kitchen. She's sniffling and trying to smile through her sniffles. Why do you have to be like this? It's hard on the boys. But it isn't. They're still young and accepting of what people do. People are like weather to them. Some people are rain; some are windy; and some are sun and clouds.

When it's time to take me to the bus station, we get awkward. Or I get awkward. She wants things for me. I can't blame her for that. It's a female disposition. All my sisters have it, my mom, too. They can see past the next hill. They have a feeling for what Professor Cohen calls "the radical contingency of existence." Doreen's not like that, though. She's there with the radical contingency but she doesn't want anything for me. She even said that in her last letter: "You do what you do." A fatalist lover.

You take care now, Tom. Evie gives me that teary look, more feeling than can fit into a daily container. Then the little smile, almost wayward, almost to herself. I know the drill but it's not a drill.

That's the last thing it is. There's no army here. She knows how I can become a deluge. The smile is necessary, like whistling in the dark. I smile, too, or at least I try to, my face cracking and creaking.

How light and portable my pain seems now.

Who rides the bus? The people who are running the show are not on the bus. No one with a substantial bank account is on the bus. This means college students, old people, minorities of all colors, people who talk to themselves, people who don't like airplanes or trains, people who enjoy riding buses, drifters, people down on their luck, proselytizers, people who don't own a car, children who have been put on the bus by an adult and who often, for the duration of the trip, clutch a piece of paper with a phone number and name on it, people on their way to get a car, people who have forgotten that the world has moved on from *Bus Stop*, foreigners, compulsive talkers, people who like to sleep in uncomfortable positions, and vets who get a modest discount for having served their country.

Among the things I will never be is a stage director, but I wish I could take all the people on any random long-haul bus ride and use them to act out *King Lear*. Usually there's a potential Goneril or Regan— women who start complaining about the air conditioning not working or the air conditioning being too cold. There's a Kent, too, some shabby guy trying to hold onto his dignity but has a temper, who inserts himself in other people's conversations, who's sure about what's right and what's wrong. And there's a Cordelia, some college girl who seems a bit too loving for this world, who lingers for an extra second when she takes off her coat or puts it on because it seems she is checking to make sure that she is still there, who requires the gentle acuity of poetry to get from weary day to weary day, who can say "Nothing" and mean it. Or so I imagine. I've never met this Cordelia but I have to believe she is out there riding buses. She would ride buses; I'm convinced of that.

Thou art a soul in bliss.

I am a soul wearing one of my decorated cotton windbreakers, the sort of jacket my father favored. He died four years ago. I've got one of his jackets but I gave it to Amy for safekeeping. On the back of the jacket I've got on, I've written FREEDOM IS HELL. Below those words there's a peace sign that I used a stencil for. The words are lettered by hand, my hand. On the front of the jacket, I've drawn a cracked purple heart on one side and on the other the South Vietnamese flag. It took a long time because no one intended for anyone to draw on this material. It's the sort of thing my last-in-line sister, Paula, who can be brusque, told me someone in an institution would do. She's a geneticist and works in a lab for a pharmaceutical company. She's making the world a healthier place and getting paid for it.

We soldiers all pretended we were healthy and regular. Sometimes when we were doing nothing special, cleaning our M-whatevers or straightening our stuff, Knightley would look around and say like he'd just had a big deep thought, "I could use a woman." We all nodded at the obvious as we tried to be impervious. Though sorely assailed, we clung to our urges.

And I? One that slept in the contriving of lust, and waked to do it.

And I? Waiting in line at the whorehouse. Do not take a picture of me.

The jacket colors I like are light olive or taupe or khaki, not army stuff, though. I had enough of that. I don't want to join anything. I should be wearing a blanket because underneath I am naked, denuded of perquisites and prerogatives, prinked up with fortune's disfavors, radicalized. I need my own uniform, though. Nothing fancy like the satin jobs guys have with the name of some Vietnam place and their unit. My sisters, all of them, tell me they don't like my jacket. I'm hiding out in it, they say. I'm holding on to nothing. I'm taunting the world-at-large about my suffering.

I'm not arguing.

The young woman who gets on in Amarillo and sits down beside me because there are no vacant two-seaters, pulls a tissue out of her pocketbook, which is a big, rough, hippie-ish thing made of jute or hemp, and blows her nose lustily. She stuffs the tissue into a pocket then leans over to put the bag on the floor. She's wearing a scoop neck top that's a size too big. I can see her breasts, beautiful the way all breasts are beautiful. If I were prone to join any congregation, it would be the First Church of the Two Circles and Blessed Triangle.

For a while, she noodles around in the bag. She knows I'm looking. You wonder if women understand how desirable they are. They must. A world of spunk-burdened guys and there they are: chemistry, electricity, physics, biology, every inherent science careening in that yearning space between men and women, a permanent flesh fire.

Are you simple, Tom? asked Knightley. Say your prayers? Believe in happy endings? Open doors for ladies like a gentleman?

The word that stands before lust is love but the word on the other side is hate. I never saw a rape there. You never knew, when guys were talking shit, what was real and what wasn't, though worse, much worse, was what didn't get talked about, that became part of the official It-Didn't-Happen. There were those USO shows that got televised back home, guys hooting and cheering, stars doing their morale-building bit, but there were shows that didn't get televised.

I wish there was one all-purpose scream in my head but there isn't. There is the girl coming toward me screaming but there are our guys screaming about what to do next and the villagers screaming. And there is a woman miles and miles away who is down on the ground and held fast and screaming until a guy stuffs her mouth with something or kicks her hard until she stops screaming.

Got-on-in-Amarillo turns her head sideways, looks up at me and smiles. She's got what she was looking for, a book.

Presidential Elections: Strategies and Structures of American Politics.

I read that when I was in college, I say. Intro to American Political Process.

It's kind of boring, she says back. I'm an elementary education major. My name's June. She extends a solid paw. Her nails are painted a soft pink.

Tom.

You must like kids.

I do. I want to have a bunch of them. But later. First, I want to teach them.

Across the aisle a burly guy wearing overalls, who takes up more like a seat and a half, burps. Then he farts.

June giggles. She must be around twenty or so. Where are you headed, Tom?

Chicago.

That's a city I'd like to see. I have a list of cities I want to see. I haven't been anywhere yet beyond Texas and Oklahoma.

They're big places.

They are. Texas is too big. You can drive all day and not leave the state. I'm from Amarillo.

Everyone has to come from somewhere.

She cocks her head at me like I said something thoughtful. And where do you come from?

Out East.

No place in particular? She's got a serious look on her face. This is a conversation with a grown man who's not her father or uncle.

Near Boston. I don't get back there too often.

And you—

A most poor man, made tame to fortune's blows.

She looks at the front of my jacket which I've got zipped up. It's October and the bus doesn't have any heat on. It doesn't seem to bother June but I'm cold.

Were you there?

I was.

Outside the bus windows, the landscape is dotted with modest displays of commerce—feed supply stores, groceries, used car lots.

Beneath the endless sky, little houses cower, one more human irrelevancy. Even in daylight, the land, subdued and ordered into tracts and farms, whimpers with desolation. *I fought for this* is a thought that's bound to go through a head. I fought for chuck steak on sale, vinyl house siding, chain-link fences, old Chryslers marooned in front yards, and tied-up dogs. There are a fair number of such dogs, also churches: Four Square Gospel, Church of the Blood of Jesus, Sanctification Tabernacle. Some Bedlamite, someone on the way to Dover or someone passing through, sitting next to a college girl who hasn't opened her book on American elections by Polsby and Wildavsky, might wonder what kind of life was going on here. More may need saving here than souls.

What was that like? She's looking at me directly, a bit wide-eyed. Her curiosity may be something more than vacant.

It's a long story and one—in any case—I don't like to tell. It's hard to tell stories where people die. It's not like a made-up story. Real people died and were hurt, lots of them and not just our guys.

I see. She tries to constrict her broad, sunny face to show how she sees, setting her mouth in a serious pucker. Her lips are painted a darker pink than her nails. She has a generous body to go with her broad face.

Don't fall, Tom.

Do you know what Bedlam is?

She shakes her head.

Bedlam was a hospital for the insane in London. People who stayed there were Bedlamites. The place was actually called Bethlehem but the way people said the word, it came out "Bedlam." Where I was, over there, it was Bedlam sometimes. People screaming, bullets, bombs. You get the picture?

Now she's leaning in closer to me. You don't have to talk. I'm sorry for asking.

> A dog ran down a lane
> Sniffed at a corpse.
> Tell me how you feel
> Emote, explain.

What are thou that dost grumble there in the northbound bus? Come forth.

You go to church? I ask her.

She draws back. I was raised Baptist but I haven't gone much lately.

Sometimes I want to go into one of these churches but they're never open when I pass by. I could use some absolution.

She draws a little further back. It's been good talking with you. I'm going to read my book now. It's something isn't it, how we've got an election coming up? Her voice is chipper like she's not giving up on me, like she's excited about another national round of lies, boasts, calumnies, and evasions.

Time shall unfold what plighted cunning hides.

It is something, I say. It is.

Even when we're not electing a president, democracy is at work, she says.

Maybe she is excited.

I look out the window, waiting for a clue about this spacious geography and its flag poles. I look harder while June settles into the two-party system. I've never registered to vote. I don't intend to.

Late October feels like the morning after summer, the air tinged with cool determination, people turning around and wondering where this came from. I've tended to be more the grasshopper than the ant. My life fits into my duffel. It's not like I've got a lot to store up or attend to. I admire ants, though, unless they want to bite you. You spend time on the ground, you wind up considering the insect kingdom.

Set ratsbane by his porridge.

The dying, dun colors outside my window agree with my jacket and my mind. I could sink into one big brown funk and stay there.

Instead, I make a show of fishing around in my duffel. June looks over and smiles a faint, distracted smile. Probably the role of third parties or negative advertising or media manipulation has her by the ass. What happened to the rank and file? So my dad, a union man, used to lament. It's all kingpins, these days. Everyone scraping his nose on the floor in front of some kingpin, he'd say while on his way to the sports page. My piss and vinegar old man who paid his son precious few compliments. My Gloucester. I miss him.

The trick of that voice I do well remember.

In my lap I have a bundle of letters, each one in its envelope. They're letters to me from my family when I was over there, also some high school buddies, one guy from college and a couple of former girlfriends. Except for my family, there was only one letter apiece from everyone else, a how-you-doing-over-there-I-remembered-you-exist kind of letter. I wrote back to each one and told them how I was doing. That's probably why they didn't write back—the-better-not-to-know-this department. If you have a farm in Vietnam and a house in hell, sell the farm and go home.

My wits begin to turn.

I don't have to read the letters. Like the play, I know practically every word in them. You need some things to hold onto, though. People who don't have mementoes scare me. They haven't seen feelingly.

I would have liked to have talked with my dad about the play but that would have been more than either of us could handle. When he asked me about what got me through, I told him it was buddies like Knightley and luck. He seemed okay with that. Like almost everyone, Dad saw things the way they show it in the movies: different guys who come together to kill an enemy they know next to nothing about but who is bad because they're the enemy. Some guys die but not too many guys. Some have sensitive lines to speak, most don't.

None of the guys is clutching a paperback *King Lear*. And none of the guys has a screaming girl advancing toward him. "Stop," the guy hollers. "Stop." What's their word for *stop*? She keeps heading toward him. She lifts an arm.

Nothing prepares you for the other side of the world because it's not only the other side of the world. It's the other side of any life you've known. *Nothing can be made out of nothing,* but Lear, as usual, was wrong. What's made out of the nothing you didn't know is vast, too large for one man, maybe too large for even one humongous nation. It dwarfs experience, knowledge, and story-telling. It empties you out because everything you've been told before is useless. What rushes in to fill you is hopeless.

I will preserve myself.

My dad was the one in our family who said I should go: it was my duty. My mom got angry with him, real angry. "Tom's blood will be on your hands," she told him. He yelled back about standing tall, about how a woman couldn't understand, about not leaving it up to the next guy.

It? What big resolute noun have I carried on my precarious shoulders? Liberty, democracy, America?

Words sauce our actions, cloud our vacant motions.

June's napping, her political science book perched precariously on her left thigh. I'm tempted but leave it there. No use messing with the electoral process.

She starts to wake up a little before we hit Oklahoma City. Her face soft from sleep, she stretches and sticks her chest out. Terrible to be in an enclosed space with that chest—Tom sits on his hands, blankets his loins.

It's been nice to meet you, Tom. I want you to know that I appreciate your sacrifice.

You're welcome, June. Stick with that book. We need all the informed voters we can get. I wink at her.

She winks back.

Every person you meet on the bus is a door. Some open wide, some not at all, some part of the way. You ask yourself what it would be like to spend time with the person who sits down next to you. You never know what's there. Most of the time you wouldn't want to. June seems like what you see is what you get. I like what I see—full of that good female sap. She'll marry, have those kids. Whether she sees Chicago doesn't really matter.

In the restroom in Oklahoma City, I splash some water on my face. I've seen other people do it. It might work for me.

The guy next to me, who's around my age, asks if I'm looking to go swimming. His voice is good-natured, no harm intended. I hear some South in his voice, maybe Tennessee. He looks at my jacket. Tryin' to wake up after 'Nam? He asks.

I keep splashing. How about you?

I'm in rehab for rehab.

That bad?

Worse. And if you don't mind my saying, our shit is getting old. There's new shit on the way. Like yuppies. I got my ass almost blown off so there could be yuppies?

So out went the candle, and we were left darkling.

Some water is dribbling down my chin. Once more, I assay the hazards and pleasures of instant camaraderie. I think of my high school grammar book: To whom am I speaking? I don't say that, though.

Has he never before sounded you in this business?

I'm going to visit one of my sisters, I say. No paper towels around so I wipe my chin with my jacket cuff.

My family's packed it in. They did their bit. I did mine. The twain weren't meeting.

Five minutes for number 286, Chicago-bound, a loudspeaker booms. He's got a duffel too, one of the army's.

I'm headed there with you. Going to see a woman.

Welcome aboard, I say.

I let him on before me. I want to see how he walks. Guys who were in the jungle walked soft and soundless. Knightley said he was going to be a ballerina after the war. This guy clomps. I wonder what kind of jungle he was walking through. Then again, maybe he's got some metal in those legs.

Your wheels in the shop? I ask.

DUI took my license. I wasn't kidding about the rehab stuff.

He's a tall, thin man with very pale skin, almost a blue tinge to his face. Something's been eating at him. Or maybe he always looked like that, a skinny, pallid kid standing on the edge of the playground watching the other kids tumble and run.

He looks out the window.

Maybe I got into our stuff too fast. Everybody else—and he looks away from the window toward the other people on the bus, which is about half full—just starts gabbing about where they're from and what the weather is like there and how these seats could be more comfortable.

It's their prerogative, I say. It's what we fought for—freedom to gab.

> No port is free, no place
> That guard and most unusual vigilance   .
> Does not attend my taking.

It's their what? He asks but then dismisses my word with a quick hand flip.

I don't get it, he says. I mean I do get it. You hold a dying man in your arms—and it happened to me, I was a medic—and you don't forget it. You ever hold a dying man in your arms?

No. I've held some other dying. Chickens, a child, hope, faith— sounds kind of random but really not random at all.

He's looking straight ahead. I doubt if he heard me. You don't forget, he says. His voice has moved into a very earnest gear. A hand punches the air. And what thanks do you get for it? That's what ticks me off. What thanks do I get? I was there and what thanks do I get for what I carry around inside me?

I'm looking at Mr. Thin Man from the corner of my eye. What performance am I beholding here? One drama is always intruding on another. Even back then, Shakespeare wasn't the only guy writing plays. You hold it against them? I ask.

I used to. I used to real bad. I couldn't do much in the world because I held it against them, their innocent dumbness. I wanted to set fire to the newspaper every morning. I wanted to walk up to people and start asking them what the fuck they thought they knew because they didn't know anything.

And?

It's not like I got on the yellow brick road and straightened out. It's more like I gave up. They won. I'm the one who's supposed to give it up.

Get on with life.

Yeah, get on with life. If I've heard it once, I've heard it four million times. People say it like nothing could be simpler.

We've come to the silent place where our lives dangle like a lynched man no one has bothered to cut down. I exaggerate but I don't.

Name's Ed. And you?

Tom.

How about sharing some of this? Make the trip a little smoother. Ed pulls a pint of Jim Beam from his duffel, opens it and takes a whiff. We go back and forth with the bottle. If faced with a choice, I prefer weed but you don't want to make someone drink alone.

Ed lets go of the war and starts telling me how much he likes to fish and wonders whether I fish and how there's nothing like fishing, which creates an agreeable word drone that meshes with the Bourbon. I'm thinking I should start a trading card collection of the people I've met on buses—Tom's Furtive All-Stars—when an old woman who's seated across the aisle and who's been looking at us not-so-furtively turns to the front and raises her hands to her mouth, megaphone style: Driver, stop this bus! These men are drinking alcoholic beverages! They are breaking the law! Arrest them immediately!

She doesn't look at us but repeats everything in case the driver didn't hear. Her voice, for someone who looks frail, is surprisingly strong, a cave of wind within her.

Lady, the driver says. I'll take care of it.

Now! The old woman shouts. Now! They are breaking the law.

Ed, who's on the aisle, leans over. We're vets, Grandma. You shouldn't call out the law on vets.

I don't care if you're cocker spaniels, she says. You have no business with that open bottle on this bus.

What if we finish it? Ed asks.

Don't get smart with me, you whippersnapper.

Who wound up her clock? I wonder to myself.

Then the driver is pulling the bus off the highway onto some kind of turn-out where a couple of semis are parked. It's gotten dark. I'm not sure where we are. I could start to get a bad, weepy feeling.

The driver puts on his brake, turns on the lights inside the bus and walks down to us.

Why don't you give me that bottle, boys, and I'll give it back to you when you leave this bus? He tries to smile a tough guy smile but doesn't have the heart. He seems nothing so much as tired. He has that haggard look of someone who's had too much to do with the human race at-large.

Ed takes one more pull and hands the bottle over. Not much left, he says.

Aren't you going to make them get off the bus, the old woman asks. It's not a question, though. She feels he should get rid of us now. Drink is evil! She shouts.

The driver looks at her dully. Calm down, madam. We have a schedule to keep to. I've already lost minutes. Let's all get along so we can get to Chicago. Okay?

Good thinking, says Ed. He turns and gives the old woman a shit-eating grin.

She says nothing. I think I hear her grinding her teeth. She has on a hat with a little veil like Mamie Eisenhower used to wear. I can't imagine Mamie stopping a bus, though. She seemed to keep her convictions to herself.

May not an ass know when the cart draws the horse? Is Ike going to play golf tomorrow? Do bears shit in the woods? Truths of my long-ago childhood.

The driver tips the brim of his cap to the woman, a show of courtesy. He shuffles toward the front of the bus with the bottle safe in hand. I'm not imagining that this man is tired. Then bus noises start to comfort us—brake being released, engine starting up, metal bulk moving. A couple people sigh: life is back to being predictable.

Maybe we should light up a joint, Ed says, and start a riot.

Right and wrong, I say.

About what? Ed asks.

There's this line that's always traveling through life, the right and wrong line. My father said that we fought the right war in the wrong place. I was in the right place but at the wrong time, Doctor John said.

Doctor John, Ed says. One out-there dude. Ever been to New Orleans? Ed's voice is mellow from the booze.

The thing is that the line doesn't stay still and everyone has their own line. I can feel the alcoholic wisdom in my own voice. Sometimes the lines line up but that's because the choices are so few, like right and wrong. We all go down this sorry chute when we have to choose.

Our posts shall be swift and intelligent betwixt us.

So you don't want to choose? You can't be with every chick in the world. There's some choosing right there. Ed clicks his tongue to confirm his smarts.

Thou, sapient sir, sit here.

The right and wrong, it takes it out of me, because everyone thinks they're right. No one thinks they're wrong. King Lear's daughters think they're right.

King Who?

It's a play by Shakespeare and two of the king's daughters are nasty to him, more than nasty really.

You think about what goes on in some play?

Well, yeah, I do. I thought a lot about it when I was over there and I keep thinking about it.

You're the first person, Tom, I ever met like that, walking around thinking about a play. Congratulations. Ed extends a hand in my direction.

You don't think about this stuff, about right and wrong?

41

I think plenty about it. I'm a bastard. My dad fathered fifteen kids with six different women. He never married one of them. People use the word "stud" but my dad was the man. I don't think the lady across the aisle would have a high opinion of him. A lot of the time, I can't say I've had a high opinion of him. He wasn't what the world calls a good father. He just liked making women pregnant and they liked getting pregnant by him. My mom says he was "a force of nature." If you're a force of nature, I guess you're right in some deep ways. You're doing what nature wants you to be doing.

You're using the past tense, I say.

He died of a heart attack last year. Not in bed, though. Ed laughs.

The old woman across the aisle looks over at us.

Good evening, I say to her. *Buona sera. Guten Nacht. Bon Soir.*

She turns her head away.

I gotta go to the can, I say to Ed.

Be my guest. He balls up his jacket and puts it behind his head. Siesta time, he says.

The bathroom, the size of a coffin, reeks of Lysol and cigarettes. Someone threw up in here not long ago, too. There's graffiti on the walls: The War is Over, White People Rule, Blow Me, a misshapen heart with the name Karen in it. The scrawling run of humankind.

Better Thou Hadst Not Been Born. Kill Kill Kill Kill Kill. Mortality Smells.

I sit on the toilet seat and put my head between my legs. Back here, the bus seems to sway like a train. Or I'm swaying inside myself. I do the take-a-deep-breath thing. I think of people I love. The feeling wells up and I'm sniffling, a tightness in my chest, but not letting go because I'm afraid of what's behind there. If I let go, I might not be left. I might wash away.

> And let not women's weapons, water drops,
> Stain my man's cheeks.

Someone raps briskly on the door. Duh, duh-duh-duh-duh, duh-duh.

42

I have full cause of weeping.

In a minute, I say. I'm in a play. I don't say that. I'm in a life. I don't say that either.

Knightley said, I think that girl was blind, the way she was walking, sort of running, sort of stumbling. I think she was blind. She never saw us. The people were yelling to tell us that she was blind.

Ed's dozed off. He snores about every fifth breath. You sleep near a lot of guys in barracks and tents and you get a sense of how sleep is different for each person. You do some listening you never wanted to do.

We lay over in St. Louis for hours. Something's wrong with the bus and there isn't another bus around to replace this one. Stay put, the driver says. Ed wakes up but falls back asleep. I fall asleep, too, but wake up when our bus, which has been fixed, pulls out and crosses the Mississippi.

Wish someone would fix me, a woman in the seat ahead of us says.

The old woman who wanted to arrest us is gone. Probably she needed to get to a church.

I pull out Professor Cohen's address. If I get off this bus and take another bus, I should be able to see him at his office at the university in Urbana-Champaign. We've been corresponding for a few years. I ask him questions—mostly naïve questions about why the characters do things, as if they were human beings, not characters in a play. He's okay with that. He likes it that someone cares enough to ask.

I wanted to ask him a question in person, though.

He's written a book and a lot of articles. I've read the book but it's not as interesting as the letters he writes. Too much time gets taken up in considering other people who have written books. I understand. It's why sergeants hang out with other sergeants. It's a fraternity. It's distracting, though, because in the hubbub about what this one admires and what that one notices or observes or considers or reconsiders, you can forget the play. What's meant to take you further in can leave you standing in right field.

It's a living, as my dad would say.

> Your critic embraces fashions, then contemns 'em
> Invents conceits, then discards 'em
> Ever plays the brave reliant voice
> At one with genius that's not his own.

Ed's up. We both are getting off at Bloomington. His woman friend, who lives in Peoria, is coming to pick him up. We talk about how Richard Nixon used Peoria as the location of Real Middle America. Ed says that Peoria is even worse than that.

It's antiseptic and pestilent at the same time. She needs to move. Does she know that?

She will after I see her. He gives me a badass wink.

When we both have our duffels ready and the bus has stopped, Ed gives me a poke, somewhere between playful affection and brusque not-affection.

Look, Tom, the Vietnam stuff I told you.

Yeah?

It was a lie. He waves the poking hand in the air as if to dispel something. I was never there. It's fucked up that I talked like that. I had a brother who was there. That's the truth. He didn't do much, though. He was some kind of supply guy who made a lot of money on the black market.

Ed puts his hand down and looks me full on. I think it's some story I want to tell because my own story isn't much of a story. Booze isn't much of a story. It's fucked up. I'm sorry. The other stuff, though, is true, like about my father having all those kids. And this woman who's driving over from Peoria, that's true.

Thanks for telling me, I say. We're making our awkward way to the bus's open front door.

You're welcome.

Here is courtesy and kind regard.

Outside, he squints in the morning sun, puts the duffel down and raises a hand over his eyes, scout-style. She drives a Dodge Charger, he announces, some kind of pale blue color, a girl's color. Nice interior, though, nice seats.

Hey, Ed.

Yeah.

Probably better not to lie in the first place. Vietnam's nothing to lie about.

He looks full on at me again but he's squinting so his face looks agitated.

Go with God, he barks at me, turns around and heads toward the parking lot.

Strip thy own back.

He turns around and flashes the peace sign, then gives me the finger, then flashes the peace sign, then turns and resumes walking.

I say to myself out loud, I've got a bus to make.

A young couple nearby overhears me and look at one another quickly. People who talk to themselves may be trouble.

Don't I know it?

Diesel exhaust—it could make me sick fast—swirls and pools around me but the little terminal that is a poor excuse for a building is not many steps away. I heft my bag.

The bus for the university leaves in an hour or so. I eye the clock on the cinder block wall, contemplate the last apple Evie gave me along with some now-crumbled rice cakes and decide to call Doreen who probably hasn't left for work yet. She's a veterinary technician, which means, as she's told me more than once, she loves innocence and instinct. People, in comparison, are muddled.

Like me, you mean?

Like you.

She likes my muddle, though. Sometimes she loves it. It's a real muddle. Some days, according to her, it has an extravagance to it, like something out of a play. Other days, it does nothing more than get on her nerves.

45

He gives the web and the pin, squints the eye and makes the harelip; mildews the white wheat, and hurts the poor creature of earth.

We've circled around one another for a long time. Though there is no contest going on, her hurt may be as large as mine. Childhood can bend iron much less mere flesh.

I have a picture in my wallet of her and Knightley and me hanging out in some bar in Washington. We're all smiling, happy to be with one another.

The phone rings a bunch but no Doreen.

What are you there? Your names?

Veteran of a Foreign War, Wayfaring Pilgrim, Underemployed Caucasian, Metaphysical Roustabout, Spiritual Lay About, Chief Player in a Minor Masque, Witness of His Own Dereliction, Erstwhile Finger on a Trigger, Recipient of Nightmares, Idler, Mountebank.

Don't flatter yourself, I can hear Doreen saying.

The professor's office is what you'd expect—a metal desk, two chairs (a comfortable one for the professor and an uncomfortable one for the visitor), a thriving corn plant and a not-thriving philodendron, a bleached and curled poster for some scholarly conference, and a lot of books.

The professor is what you'd expect, too: a small, rumpled man with a deeply creased forehead. He looks as though he's been cogitating forever. He has on heavy black glasses. His shoes, which are also black and could use a shine, look heavy, too. He's been pulling his share of the weight, maybe more than his share.

Pleased to finally meet you, Tom. He waves at the uncomfortable chair. Glad you made your way here. I don't get many letters such as yours.

Tom's wandered here and there, hither and yon. Tom's been shot at. Tom's heard worse. Tom's sat in church and waited. Tom's seen the girl coming toward him. She had on one of those small cone-shaped hats. Something was in her hand.

So, Professor.

Call me Mike.

So, Mike, why does Cordelia have to die?

You don't beat around the bush, do you?

I could ask how the weather's been.

Spit fire, spout rain. I quote from memory. We don't need pleas-
antries and banalities, plenty of that to go around already. The news
is not news. He waves again, this time at the daily paper that's lying
face up on his desk. Serviceable villains. What do you think, Tom?
He pulls a Pall Mall from a pack but doesn't light it.

I think it's more than she's too good for this world. I think it's
more than this world being unbearable.

Mike says nothing. I'd say he's frowning but that seems his permanent expression. His eyes, though, have a crinkly light in them.

Cordelia, Mike says, dies because Edmund has given an order.
The various hells that are unleashed occur because Lear makes a deci-
sion—before we ever meet him—and executes it. Human beings do
things then there are consequences. Words, however, are actions. Lear
doesn't tramp around and carve up his kingdom with some surveyor
like Henry David Thoreau at his side. He speaks. Edmund's order is
written. Carry it so as I have set it down.

Mike taps his Pall Mall on his ugly metal desk.

Edmund tries to take it back but it's too late. We have to accept
the consequences. We can't wave a wand and undo our words and
decisions. Fairy tales wave wands but the play is an anti-fairy tale.
Everything gets worse. There is no magical *but* that emerges and
makes everything right.

A fairy godmother, I say.

Yes, a fairy godmother. In the comedies, there are such people who help to sort out the confusions and misapprehensions
that are causing consternation. In the tragedies, people, one way
or another, are bound to fall, but they cause their own grief. No
one makes Lear divide his kingdom. No one makes Othello listen
to Iago or Macbeth listen to his wife. No one makes Hamlet

dither. Shakespeare shows how free we are and how unable we are to deal with that freedom. Mostly we dither along, ill with our purposes, and call it a life. Shakespeare doesn't let his tragic heroes get away with that.

Mike? I say. So Cordelia dies because malice is boundless?

Edmund has his reasons, Tom. Everyone has his reasons. That's a human prerogative. You've told me some about you and the war. We had our reasons. They—North and South—had their reasons. We explain ourselves over and over. Equalities are so weighed. Is it more than this world being unbearable? What is that *more*?

He remembers his cigarette and lays it on top of a pile of books then picks it up and lights it with a Zippo he pulls from his pants pocket.

I'm not supposed to do this, he says, and shoots out some smoke.

It used to bother me a lot, I say, that Cordelia dies. More than a lot. I'd lie there at night and think about how sad it is, how awful it is to see Lear holding her body, but lately it doesn't bother me as much. I don't know if that's good or bad. I lean forward and put my head down. It might start bothering me again, though. It's like that. Like a tide.

Tom?

I don't say anything. I'm fighting back the tears, a literal expression if there ever was one.

Mike blows out more smoke and then crushes his cigarette in the philodendron pot.

Forgiveness is a story we tell ourselves because we have to have that story. It may not be a true story but that doesn't matter. What matters is that we can imagine it. If we can imagine it, we may be able to do it. I stress the *may*.

I'm still bent over but I'm listening.

You're not going to get to take a deep breath, Knightley said, before you pull the trigger. It doesn't work like that. Crazy is crazy.

Mike stands up, walks the two steps over to me and puts a hand on my shoulder. I guess we jumped too soon into the deep end of the pool.

That's why I came here—to jump. My voice is choked.

He picks his hand up. I've been teaching this play for over thirty years. It's a strange way to spend your life. A hundred years ago I'd have been a rabbi, maybe, in some little town in Poland. Now I'm a professor. Who knows what, a hundred years from now, people will be doing? Shakespeare had these stories from the past. They were like voices calling out to him. There was this king who divided his kingdom. There was this loving daughter. There was this man who had two sons, one legal, one illegal. But the strongest voice is the one that wants to believe and that voice never goes away.

Her lips seem to move.

That's so sad.

That's so sad.

I've picked my head up. Somehow, this is what I expected. And I'm thankful. And I tell the professor that.

He makes a little awkward laugh. This doesn't happen every day. That's good for both of us. Sometimes I ask myself, how did this man named Shakespeare get to this place, the place at the end of *Lear*. But I suspect you know something about that, Tom.

A little, I say.

The riddle—Mike walks over to the one window in his office—is not so much the ending but our going on. I don't mean that the impulse to stay alive is a riddle but that our reasons are riddles inside of riddles. All those riddles in the play that the fool proposes, why are they there? It's not comic relief. The fool isn't very funny at all. The fool sees through our going on. Mike leans forward a bit and almost presses his forehead against the window then turns to me. I love the fool. He's nameless. He's generic. He's amused but amusing. He knows a spirit when he sees one. He won't take yes for an answer. His every tangent is a salient.

He unreasons reason. Mike heaves an existential sigh. But that's probably enough for one day.

We shake hands and he gives me his home phone number. If you need to talk, ring me up, he says. Just no collect calls. Ask for the King Lear Hotline if my wife picks up. She'll get it. I've told her about you. If my son picks up, tell him to do his homework. And by the way, that's quite a jacket you have.

My steps down the stairs to the first floor make a weird echo, as if there's no one else in the building. For some fugitive seconds, I think about how I could have gone back to school. Then I think better. If only school were for fools.

Poor Tom hath been scared out of his good wits.

The midday bus to Chicago is about half full. I put my duffel on the seat beside me to discourage any chatty wayfarers.

My head's expanded but not exploded.

> I went to see the doc.
> He rang my mind.
> Arrant words turn
> A seeker blind.

Riding the bus gives you time to contemplate the works of man, specifically the American version. No one pretends that any of it has any value in and of itself. Stores are stores. They exist to sell stuff and America has a whole lot of stores. Even the churches are stores that are advertising Jesus. I watch the churches go by with their zippy, punning sayings out front. Fight Truth Decay, Read the Bible. Free Trip to Heaven, Details Inside. Hang Out With Jesus, He Hung Out For You. Weather Report: God Reigns, the Son Rises.

The fool says some zippy stuff but there's that undertone of anguish. What is Lear doing? What is everyone doing? Then again, no one gets saved in *King Lear*. No one waves a wand.

My sister Amy lives in a suburb with her husband Hank and their three kids. Amy's a nurse, Hank's a lawyer. Once you've said what people do with their days to make money, you've said what needs to be said. If Amy likes to go to a park and release balloons, if Hank likes to make chocolate fondue, that stuff isn't what gets said. We're here to work in America.

Tom was a guy who went to Vietnam and afterward had a hard time getting his life together. Got stuck in the mire. Or he was the mire.

I wonder how many auto parts stores there are on the way to Chicago. Would you die for Mufflers-on-Sale-This-Week? It wasn't an idle question for me. Would you die for Dairy Queen, A&W Root Beer, Burger King?

You're missing the point, Tom.

Tom has to become someone else. I became a soldier. Then I wasn't a soldier. I was back to being—but what was I? Veteran? That's not much of a category. Edgar was the son of a nobleman. It's not like he was doing much of anything. He was born and that made him something. Then he was un-born. It's not something I'd confide to someone who sat down next to me on a bus but that's what happened—I was un-born.

Come, unbutton here.

Whatever I was, I was no longer. I didn't become anything, though. Or I became a sort of sieve. Someone who could say shit happens, or he bought it, or fuck this war, but who lived in quiet terror. If you think no one can be in quiet terror for months and months, you're wrong. Just because you're going to Burger King doesn't mean other people aren't swallowing old rats and eating cow dung. You just don't want to know about them. And I wouldn't blame you.

What are we dying for? Knightley asked. Dying for the right to pussy. Dying for some pussy, too, right about now. We all laughed, even me, the un-born sieve.

Mistress Input, His Hardness entreats you—open your gates.

On the worried-about-my-brother-Tom meter, Amy comes in around medium. Part of her is it's-his-life-and-he's-entitled-to-do-what-he-wants-to-do-with-it. If he wants to ride on buses and pretend he's actually doing something, then he's entitled to. But part of her is what-happened-to-him?

She's asked me and I've tried to tell her, but she comes from The Land of Rules where you Do This and Get That.

A woman is standing by my duffel bag seat. Mind if I sit here?

We must have stopped somewhere. A few people must have gotten on. There are open pairs of seats on the bus, though.

> Here sits one for whom time fell apart.
> The strutting days no longer counsel me

If that's what you want, I say.

That's what I want. She smiles a slightly off center smile and puts a hand up to her hair to do that reassurance thing women do with their hair—a comforting, alluring pat. She's wearing a dress that is more like a sheath. I'd say she's around my age. All she has with her is a little pocketbook, one of those ones with a big metal catch on the top of it. She plunks it in her lap and does a little seat adjustment shuffle that involves skirt tugging and rustling her behind. Being a woman is a full-time job.

I've asked Professor Mike whether Lear's big problem was that he didn't get women. He didn't understand his daughters, whether they were good, bad, or indifferent. He was busy being a guy, a king guy. He thought women were men. Or he didn't think about it at all. He was disappointed with his daughters but isn't disappointment something we create on our own?

The professor thought I was exaggerating. At the beginning of the play, before Lear starts feeling that his daughters are a bunch of ingrates, he doesn't have anything special to say about them. They're his daughters and that's that—like they're off in some harem or nursery. But then look at Gloucester. He had son problems. Maybe it's just being a parent, no matter whether you've got sons or daughters.

Sometimes the professor holds his cards too tight to his chest. Why does Lear need his daughters to protest their love? What's with that? The king doesn't trust women's feelings but he needs to hear how they love him.

Sing me a silent song.

My name's Gwendolyn, she says. Don't call me Gwen or Lynn. She extends an unringed hand.

How many things are wrong with this picture? Not that it bothers me.

I take her hand and try to smile. It's a small hand but I feel a tingle because it's a woman's hand. Pleased to meet you, Gwendolyn. I'm Tom.

Who hath had three suits to his back, six shirts to his body.

That's a lovely dress, I say, because it is.

It's vintage. I like to dress like a woman not a eunuch. Feel the rayon. She's taken back her hand but thrusts her arm out.

I touch and tingle some more. You a little cold in that?

I'm warm-blooded, she says.

I can feel my cold self heating up.

Every woman used to dress like a woman, she says. I'm an actress so I get to dress up anyway but I can dress up every day. I think that's beautiful. And I think your jacket is beautiful. Were you there?

I was.

It couldn't have been easy.

It wasn't. I've let go of her sleeve, though I didn't want to. Whatever I could say about female softness would not be enough. A number of bad choices beckon. You on your way to do some acting?

I'm on way to audition back East, in New York. A Tennessee Williams play.

I'm waiting for her to unload something on me—money, desperation, confidences. Instead, she asks me my age.

Thirty-two.

I'm thirty-one. I don't lie about my age the way some actresses do. It's not good to get old when you're an actress.

You don't look old. Aside from a few small frown lines, she looks like the plump of life. You travel on the bus often?

Only when I'm down on my luck or it's convenient. She smiles, but not at me, more away from me.

Here it comes.

Want to know why I sat down to next to you? She doesn't pause for an answer. You're in the available seat. That's the seat on the bus that someone sits in who's available. You know about that seat, don't you?

I'd heard of it but didn't think it applied anymore, an old custom, like a king having a fool.

No, I say.

Well, it's true, she says. Are you available?

Are you? I ask back.

Why dost thou lash that whore? Strip thy own back.

Semi, she says. Not here, not now, but sometimes. I've been through some trouble. Not living right, not taking care of myself, listening to the wrong people. She opens the pocketbook, pulls out a tissue and dabs at her eyes.

She could be looking for a dexterous hand, a willing ear, or even some cut-rate wisdom. We Americans are all in this emotional-material stew together. President Johnson said something like that. I try to look thoughtful. I try to remember the name of a play by Tennessee Williams.

Why did you go? She asks.

Women can turn on a dime.

I didn't know what else to do.

Life's like that sometimes. It's sure not like a play where everyone knows their lines. She smiles a better smile, more from somewhere inside her not outside. She gets up, but as she does she gives me a scrap of paper with her name and a phone number on it. This is me, she says. Maybe we can talk some more sometime. I like your style.

We came crying hither.

This in Chicago? I ask.

Chicago, she says and moves toward a vacant two-seater. It's just a few steps but she flows in that dress.

I used to think that Lear wanted his male mob with him because he might get lonely. Then I thought that Lear didn't know what loneliness was. What he had to learn, though I'm not sure what Lear learned, is loneliness. It's too easy to quote about the bare forked animal. It's almost like a bumper sticker. There's loneliness when you're by yourself and there's loneliness when you're with other people. I'm not sure which is worse but I suspect Gwendolyn knows both sorts.

I fold the piece of paper and put it in a pant pocket. I've got a different sort of tingle going on, the one that includes sex but is deeper, grim lightning inside me with no place to go.

Arm it in rags, a pygmy's straw does pierce it.

When we get off the bus in Chicago, we don't acknowledge one another.

> Her boat hath a leak
> And she must not speak.

Though I'm ten or so feet from my sister Amy, she waves vigorously. Hi's and hugs and quick words about how she's in a hurry because one kid is somewhere and another kid is somewhere else and she has to be in both places and elsewhere. My head whirls. Motherly logistics. I think of our mom having four kids. When I once asked her how she did it, she said that she didn't. It did her.

I admire the recent car and the orderly, tree-lined streets we proceed down. I listen to stories about her children's successes and endearing traits. It doesn't look like I'm going to join the parental parade, so I try to pay attention and murmur the right confirming things to her. Meanwhile, I still have Gwendolyn in my head and how there always is someone else out there in life who has a half of something that might match up with your half. A half would be a lot.

Doreen has told me that I'm a romantic for thinking such things. Also, she's told me that I'm incorrigible. I guess the two go together. Still, there are a lot of people who get thrown to the side of the road and it could be your side.

Are you listening, Tom? Amy asks.

Sure. You've been telling me about your Halloween party.

I'd forgotten it's that late in October. Or I didn't know in the first place.

Frateretto calls me, and tells me Nero is angler in the lake of darkness. I've fished there, too.

It's a pre-Halloween party. Parents and their kids dress up and play games and don't drink booze. I've heard about it but never made it to one. This looks like my chance.

Amy stops to pick up one kid and then another and then stops at some friend's house. The kids are all over me with declarations and questions. I'm seven! I got a bike! I want to eat lots of chocolate on Halloween. I'm going to be a pirate. I'm going to be Cinderella. Where have you been, Uncle Tom? Was it warm there? How is Aunt Evie? Are you going to see Grandma? I wish I could go somewhere on a bus. Would you take me, Uncle Tom? Can I touch your jacket?

They're this little wave of feeling that keeps waving.

I'm going to be a little girl in a village who runs towards the GIs.

I'm going to be a lieutenant.

I'm going to be a Shakespeare professor.

I'm going to be Flibbertigibbet.

Who's that?

Flibbertigibbet is a spirit.

What's a spirit?

A spirit is something you can't see but is there.

We all think about this.

Like the wind?

Yes, like the wind. And this spirit likes to play tricks.

What kind of tricks? Can the spirit make things disappear? Can the spirit fly?

Little tricks, I say. He can make spider webs appear where there are no spiders.

Really?

If the Flibbertigibbet—that's a hard word to say, Uncle Tom—is invisible then what does he look like?

Oh, he looks a lot like me.

Like you? They start laughing. I laugh, too.

Amy opens the car door. What's so funny?

Uncle Tom is going to be a long word. He's going to be a spirit. Like the wind. He's going to tell fibs.

Amy gives me an I-love-you-brother-but look.

Hey, I say, a bit of Shakespeare to enliven the proceedings.

Who? The kids chorus.

Aroint thee, witch, aroint thee!

I wear my boxers outside my pants which I wear inside-out along with a shirt that's inside-out. I randomly smear my face with charcoal and wear a kerchief around my forehead. I'm barefoot, too. The kids are very pleased with me. Amy is a car hop waitress in a short skirt. She has some sort of paper tiara in her hair. Hank is an old-time baseball player. They're serious costumers.

We bob for apples, play bingo, and tell ghost stories. I stay away from the ghost stories but win two bingo cards.

Various moms and dads talk to me about who I might be and I patiently explain about Flibbertigibbet. They start talking about when they read *King Lear* or talk about how they didn't read *King Lear*.

It's a tragedy, isn't it? One mom asks me. She's dressed as some-thing like Pocahontas. She's got braids and a headband and is wearing moccasins. I never read it because tragedy frightens me.

It can be frightening, I say. The end is very unhappy. Actually, it's beyond unhappy. But the character I'm dressed as is more like a goofy spirit.

Goofy?

Ties people's shoe laces together, that sort of thing.

More like the joker in the last row of study hall in high school?

Sort of. People back then, in Shakespeare's time, had a lot of belief in spirits. And the play takes place even way before Shakespeare's time so those people had even more belief in spirits.

She puts a caramel in her mouth and starts that slow chewing. Do you believe in spirits?

Absolutely. I've seen them.

Really? Her jaw is working hard. Where?

Oh, here and there. That's how it is with spirits. Here and there. They don't work a day job.

Amy walks over. My brother feeding you some line, Clarisse?

Several, actually, but I like them. She swallows the last of her candy.

I start thinking of Gwendolyn. I wonder who she would dress as. I wonder about her undressed.

The afternoon gently swoons. Sugary children and their imagination-besotted parents depart. We are but poor players, I don't say. Instead, I help clean up spilt cider and soda, candy wrappers, and bits of pretzels, chips, and the orange dust that cheese doodles give off, while Amy tells me about this friend and that friend. Someone just got divorced; someone is getting divorced: the piercing but small-scale fracases. No grandiloquent land wars in Asia.

I head upstairs to reverse my reversed clothes. It's good I wore boxers on the inside, too. Then I call Gwendolyn from the phone on the hall landing on the second floor. I don't expect her to answer. I don't even expect the number to be a working number.

Gwendolyn?

Yes.

This is Tom from the bus.

Tom from the bus?

The guy you talked to on the way to Chicago. You talked about Tennessee Williams.

Actually, the play I'm auditioning for is by a contemporary playwright but you wouldn't know his name. Everybody knows

Tennessee. It's much easier to tell people that. Not that there's anything reassuring about Tennessee Williams.

You busy tonight?

I've been memorizing lines and waiting for my sister to go out on the date she's been telling me about since I got here. You aren't Mr. Right are you?

No way. I'm not Mr. Wrong. I'm just not Mr. Right.

My VA shrink would be proud of me. Define yourself in a realistic but positive light, Tom. That's how self-esteem grows, from positive light.

That's a relief, she says. A big build-up never works out.

Too much positive light, I say.

What?

> Prefer the dark
> When candles die
> And owls return
> Before dawn's spark.

Nothing, just a joke to myself.

Just because I sat next to you on the bus – you're not going to be squirrelly are you?

She's thinking about what's wrong with my picture. No, I say. She doesn't say anything but then says, Well I guess you're okay.

I get directions and tell her I'll be by soon. I feel like a kid, back before college and the war. I even have to ask for the car.

Hank still has on his old-time jersey, New York Giants. We talk about Mel Ott for awhile. He hit some balls that never came down.

Don't smoke dope in the car, Tom. Okay? Hank's a direct sort.

I wouldn't think of it.

You would, that's why I'm telling you.

You think all we did was smoke reefer?

No, I'm sure you went to the whorehouse and drank a few beers.

Flibbertigibbet is naturally high. And with that he gives me the keys.

On the way there—another suburb not too far from Amy's but not as posh—I have to pull over because I start hyperventilating.

I hate myself. I hate my twittering words. I hate myself for letting myself go to war. I hate myself for continuing to live, for not dying. I hate myself for not being able to stay in one place, for moving from town to town and mood to mood and acting like I'm more or less okay when I'm not.

Let it out, the VA guy says but I have and it's not gone. It's not a glass of water you pour down a drain. I am the drain.

I shake some. What I know is how alone I am, sitting in my brother-in-law's Volvo amid toys and an array of cellophane litter. Way to go, Tom. Way to stay, Tom.

I hate that there are people standing around at the end of the play, trying to say something. Hell is never enough. And I'm one of those people, full of sententious crap, obeying the weight of this sad, ongoing time.

You're being too hard on yourself, Tom. Is there any other way to be? There is, the VA guy says. It's like this, you get up in the morning and you do some meaningful work during the day, and you come home to someone who loves you. Easy. Nothing to it. Let me at it. Hey, Briggs; hey, Stone; hey, Knightley; hey Lieutenant, this is easy. Hey, girl running through the village, this is easy.

Howl.

I subside. I pick up a little rubber ball that's on the passenger-side floor and squeeze it. I'm sweaty and chilled. I should turn the car around and go back to Amy's. I don't want to unburden myself to a stranger. I will hate myself even more. I place the ball back on the floor and start up the car.

The building Gwendolyn is staying in is three-floors, brick and square. I guess you'd call it functional, without a trace of beauty or grace or other such bizarre words.

I fought for function. I fought for fast food. I fought for fear. The bumper stickers in my head. You could be making money, Tom. You got ideas.

At the front door, before I ring the bell to 3A, I try to tidy up. Hurricane hit the dude but he's tidying up. No roof left but he's got a piece of flooring to stand on. Man's lucky.

Run, run, O run!

A few more deep breaths should do it. Here's the ex-soldier doing his duty. He's ministering to the wayward actresses of the world, to small children. Is there a dog around for him to pat?

She buzzes me in and has the apartment door open for me. She looks at me, looks at me again and then hugs me. It's sisterly, tender, but she doesn't let go and I start to feel she may have been sitting here crying too. She may have been shaking; she may be one of those who don't stop after the play is over. She doesn't let go. I start to hug back, but it's too desperate, but then it isn't. We're both gripping each other, holding on tightly, but then it becomes our bodies waking up to each other and not wanting to stop, and we start pressing into each other, pressing hard. We pull back our heads, and then our mouths find one another's and we're gone, we're crazy, staggering around like one body with four legs but we don't fall until a couch appears.

The after-words are quiet. We're numb with surprise. We're exhausted from a lot more than a tussle on a couch. We're thankful. And I think I can say "we." I think she would say that, too. She does.

Wow, she says, I guess we needed that.

Our clothes decorate the floor. Evie says that people are making art like that these days.

And your sister? I ask.

With any luck, she'll be out all night with Mr. Right.

You look good in a dress and you look good not in a dress. I touch her hair, which is long and dirty blonde.

I'm overweight.

You don't want to be at war with your body.

I guess I can do what I want. She gives me a playful shove that's not all playful. I'm shaky, she says. I know you're shaky, too. Two shaky people, that's not good. I need a man who isn't shaky, but who understands what shaky is. Do you think there is such a man?

Eve probably asked Adam that.

She laughs and leans into me. She puts a hand on my sex.

Once more.

I'm not all shaky, I say. We're picking up clothes.

No, you're not. Ships in the night should be ships in the night, though.

Through the sharp hawthorn blow the winds.

I haven't asked you what you do. I'm not going to. That actress stuff I said, that's only partially true. I want to be an actress. I buy and sell vintage clothes. Someone told me about this play. She stops and looks at me. You work out?

I walk a lot. And I do push-ups—my interior sergeant.

You're doing something right. You've probably got plenty of wrongs sticking to you but you're doing something right.

Thanks.

I probably talk too much, like how I sat down next to you on the bus. My sister tells me I'm needy.

That's a shitty word, 'needy.' Shakespeare would never countenance it.

Shakespeare? Countenance?

We've gathered our clothes but haven't put them on.

I could use a shower. Would your sister mind?

If there's a hair on the stall floor, she goes nuts. Be my guest. But what about Shakespeare?

It's a play I'm in, I don't say.

It's a feeling, I don't say.

It's a kind of ether we're all suspended in but we don't know it, I don't say.

I like Shakespeare, I say.

TOM o'VIETNAM

Is what it says on your jacket from Shakespeare? She's holding her clothes to her chest with one hand and lightly scratching her crotch with the other.

Freedom is hell? No. He wouldn't say something like that.

Because?

Because he never went to some place that made no sense to him and watched even less sense occur. The reasons in his world were traditional, not made up.

She's holding her clothes now with both hands. Her pubic hair is darker than her hair color. I never got Shakespeare, she says. That's kind of embarrassing because I'm trying to be an actress. It's the words, how they talk funny, and all the stuff about kings and queens. Kings and queens—that was a real long time ago.

He wrote a lot about sex, I say, pretty dirty stuff, natural but dirty. Bawdy.

She drops her clothes, puts her hands on her labia and starts to spread them while making purring sounds. Improv class, she says.

Once more.

I do shower and I do leave. We don't make promises about being in touch. We've already been in touch big time.

Shall I hear from you anon?

No.

There's a light on downstairs when I open the front door. Amy's in the kitchen wiping down the counters with a sponge. She's got on what looks like Hank's bathrobe and her hair is sticking out all over the place. She has on a pair of gray, fuzzy slippers I think she's had since high school.

Nice evening? She asks.

Someone I met on the bus.

You should go into the hospitality industry, be a greeter. Aren't you a little old—

Ease off, sister.

Sorry, just frustration and wonderment. You seem, Tom, to exist in some state of suspended something or another. There's a pile of candy bags at the end of the counter that she's working on. She lays down the sponge, pulls out a Kit Kat and offers the bag to me.

No thanks. I ate three this afternoon.

No one's counting but suit yourself. Those of us leading so-called lives sometimes wonder about those who aren't.

That sounds a lot like a judgment. I look around. The lighting's awfully bright in here. There are these things called "dimmers."

I don't blame you for changing the topic. I'm being catty. Caring does that to people. She takes a gulp of a pale liquid that looks like liquor.

Is this a library stay? She asks. She folds up the candy's paper wrapper and the silver wrapper inside that. She's not a crumpler or a baller.

I was thinking of it. Sort of a good role model for your kids. Scholarly.

As you know, they adore their strange uncle with his jacket and his duffel. They don't even think you're strange.

That's the beauty of kids, I guess.

She walks over and stands on tiptoe so she can muss my hair up. Where would I be if I didn't know that you exist?

Then there's life in't, I say.

I hope you got laid, she says.

That hasn't been my problem.

She goes back to her glass. I'd offer you something but it's not good for you.

Upstairs, I lie down on the bedroom floor. I'll mess the bed up in the morning. Tom's been here.

I like to think the librarians remember me but I doubt they do. Now and then, I'm there for a week or two. I could ask but that seems stupid. It might lead to questions, too, though librarians tend to be discreet characters. It's an inner place, a library, like a brain opened up, or like those old-time phrenology charts of people's heads where there's this going on in one place and that going on in another. People shuffle in, people stride in, people wander in: different errands. It's wanting to see what happens in Peyton Place or on a raft on the Mississippi or learn about George Westinghouse or how to raise tropical fish or it's being in high school and having to do a report on the Bonus Army or paramecium or wanting to know why a war was fought and believing a book could tell you. Just killing time, picking up this and that and letting your feet dangle in the current of moments, not driven by anything or confronting anyone or running from anyone or being proclaimed or declaiming snatches of speeches or pretending to be someone who is above it all or beyond it or beside it. A terrible thing to be a pretender, to never hold your name in your own mouth.

I'll bring him the best 'parel that I have.

I have my errands, too, for Amy, like help rake the yard and pick up her youngest at school and sort out stuff in the garage. Is he handicapped? I heard a neighbor ask her once. Not easy to explain one unsteady piece of America's commitment to keeping the world safe for democracy. And if Tom stops gnashing his teeth, his grief will stop eventually. Storms and bad nights and battles all end. Even *Lear* ends.

And there's the fact that Tom can pay for his bus tickets, that beside his string of transient jobs, his mother's brother Bob left money in his will to help someone who "stood up for America."

Living or dead, people do funny things with their money.

"That's what I want," sang the Beatles.

Who could begrudge poor Tom?

I don't read about the war I was in but I read about others. No one knows why the First World War started. Millions of people died. Vietnam was a pimple compared to that war. We're going to have this monument in Washington with names on it, but they would have had to build a monument that was miles and miles long for that war. And there were more guys who were obliterated, who were physically gone, flesh thrown to the sky or lost in the mud. Even their names were lost.

We don't learn much, Knightley said.

If anyone asks, and sometimes there are nosy and not well-intentioned people who do ask, I tell them that I'm writing a book. I'm doing research. People nod respectfully. Tom over there, the one who's got a blanket on, he's doing research. He went to college. Didn't graduate but went to college. Speaks well enough. Seems to find the words for most occasions. Carries a copy of a play by Shakespeare around with him. Homeless but smells okay. Hell-bound but known to smile. Evasive but forthright.

Shake spear, kick in the rear.

Your inconsequence commends you. Take these words and bring them to someone who can read them.

We've got our orders, the lieutenant would say. We're going into a village. We've got reports of activity. It might get hot, even if you're a-cold, it might get hot.

Good day at the library? Amy asks.

I start telling her about the British generals in the First World War and how they all should have been taken out and shot.

That sounds kind of radical, Tom. She's making some kind of casserole.

Church potluck tonight? I ask.

What would you know about it?

I know General Haig was a moron and a butcher. I know that.

Nixon had a Haig, didn't he? Would you get some ketchup for me?

What are you making?

I'm a homemaker, Tom, I know what I'm doing. Did your war have butchers?

My war?

You know what I mean. You're always making these quibbles with me.

"My war" means I possessed something. I didn't possess anything.

You've told me you carried a book around. You carried our letters around. But what about Haig?

The usual, someone who's at the top and has no sense of what the bottom looks like. Someone who tells the politicians what they want to hear, and they're afraid of him because he wears a uniform. He's a real man and they aren't.

You staying around a while?

I hope to make it to three-score and ten, maybe some extra, so I can drink a few more Wild Turkeys at the Legion Hall and talk to the young guys about the last war and the one before that one.

The enemy's in view; draw up your powers.

You're pretty wound up. Amy's about to put whatever it is she's making into the oven. I guess Haig got to you.

There aren't soybeans in that are there? Soybeans are for cattle.

You going into ranching?

I'm not staying for too long.

You can stay for as long as you want. I just asked.

I know. I should have plans. Though I don't think the fool had plans. He was a first responder, making fun, like John Lennon.

John Lennon?

I'll ask the professor and I do.

Is this the King Lear Hotline?

Yes, Tom. What can I do for you today? Have you caught me at a bad time? Let's face it: all times in Lear Time are bad times.

I motion to Amy to listen in on another line.

Why doesn't Shakespeare bother with motives? Why doesn't he tell us why Lear is dividing up his realm? Why does he talk about a "darker purpose?" And who is this "we" he's talking about at the beginning of the play? Isn't he the king? I don't see a queen anywhere.

Joey, turn down the stereo, the professor calls out. I'm on the phone. Kids, he says. What did we do to deserve rock 'n' roll?

I was just talking about John Lennon and how he was like the fool.

One of the Beatles, right? I can't speak to that but I can try to answer your questions. You can read the footnotes, so you know "darker purpose" means something like we've been keeping you in the dark, but now we're going to tell you what's up.

"Darker" is an ominous word, though, Amy says.

Who's that?

My sister Amy.

Hi, professor. Tom said I could listen in. I read *King Lear* in college.

Hello, Amy. Yes, it is an ominous word. It sets the tone for the play. It tells us about Lear's inner world too. He doesn't know who he is. He's dark inside. He's adumbrating his darkness.

Adumbrating? Amy and I both say that.

Look it up, the professor says. A couple of its meanings apply here. In any case, the "we" is a royal "we." The king is the government, the realm, and royalty, too, with all its perquisites. Does Lear acknowledge other people outside of that "we?" Professor Cohen pauses. It seems as though Joey is asking him something. I hear the words "peanut butter."

Does he? I ask. I don't think so. I don't think he gets other people at all.

That's not his job, says the professor. He's crawling toward death which constitutes a motive to divest himself of his realm. He's looking for help from "younger strengths."

Is that really a motive? I ask.

Seems good enough to me, Amy says.

I agree with your sister, Tom. You don't want to impose modern psychology on this. And the capacity of human beings to invent reasons wasn't born yesterday.

My oven timer just went off. Thanks, professor.

I'm hungry myself. Good to hear from you, Tom. Are you okay?

Never been better.

That doesn't answer my question. He hangs up.

First let me talk with this philosopher.

There's always that feeling at the end of the play, that falling into the next moment—that isn't a moment at all—but something formless and more than any human being can handle. I feel some of that when the professor hangs up. I felt a lot of that over there because I was falling. I could see myself falling, not on the ground or in the air but somewhere else, somewhere inside me.

Help me, I'd say to Knightley.

You need a hand? You need a pat on the ass? You need some home words? What the fuck do you need?

I need to be elsewhere.

And now I am, but I'm not.

I didn't know you read *King Lear*, I say to Amy.

I probably didn't communicate all my academic pursuits to my little brother. Right now I'm back to making dinner. Want to help me put together a salad?

I do.

A weird thing over there was that amid the chaos there was all that army structure; every day doing strictly what it was told to do. At first I hated that. I'd been waking up in my dorm room when I woke up and going to sleep when I went to sleep. Then I became regimented—or as regimented as uncertainty allowed, as falling allowed, as shivering allowed. So you were straight in one way but bent in another. Nothing was made up and everything was made up because the enemy wasn't part of the plan. The enemy had to be engaged.

Knightley loved that word. Got us an engagement.

I think that lettuce has to be washed, Tom. There's some grit in it.

You need to establish a routine, the VA guy told a group I was in. We looked at one another. Where do we get this routine? We'd been receivers, not initiators. Get a job was the answer on all four of the multiple test choices.

I did. I've worked in an auto parts warehouse, washed dishes, planted trees, demonstrated vacuum cleaners, clerked in two bookstores, and gave bass guitar lessons. Since I couldn't stay still, my résumé grew apace. I hadn't found myself, as more than one sister told me. There I was, reaching into a dark drawer in a dark room in a dark house. Look at this nothingness!

It's a word I've discussed via the mails with Professor Mike, the nothing coming from nothing. How did Shakespeare get to that? Was it just words, a formula? Did he know? He had to know. He had to have been to that place. Not that we'll ever know. Not that it would matter.

You're going to need the spinner for that lettuce. It's in the cabinet over the dishwasher.

I've thought that someone should stage the play in Vietnam. It could begin with a map and that meeting where the place was cut into two. The US wasn't there but we show up in the next act or so, eager to take on a world of shit about which we know nothing. We're believers, though we aren't sure what exactly we believe in beyond ourselves. That's enough to go to war, though. You can't let anyone mess with your self-respect.

Which of you shall we say doth love us most?

We were on a love mission in that war. Love us for being Americans. If you don't love us, we'll kill you. It's a death you richly deserve. It's a death you've brought on yourself. You should have listened to us, however many thousands of miles away we were, you still should have listened to us because we had something important to say. We had things to say beyond what our presidents said and our ambassadors and our secretaries of state.

Kiss my ass. Go fuck yourself. Eat shit. Die motherfucker.

Love goes bad. Ask Cordelia or the other two girls.

Lear and the fool are stumbling through the jungle. Lear looks crazy, but he's not the only one around who looks crazy. He meets a guy who's been tortured and had his eyes gouged out and left to die. He meets another guy who's a freelance fool. He's a soldier. He's AWOL. On his helmet it says Prince of Darkness.

Tom, get with it. I'm going to tell everyone we're ready to eat.

In the background of the play, mortars are going off, rounds of every caliber, helicopters are landing and leaving. You have to shout to be heard. Lear's wildness is answered by other wildness.

Look, my friend, the night explodes, these stars are ours.

Probably staging it like that is not the most practical idea, though I'll take it up with the professor. I could go back to school and study drama. I know something about conflict. Maybe I could get credits for life experience. My sister Paula has pointed that out to me. I can't say that studying appeals to me though. I wouldn't know what to do with the distance—me and my unaccredited shadow.

How many credits for sitting around and telling lies? How many credits for almost getting your ass shot off? How many credits for getting your ass shot off?

Which salad dressing do you want?

Ranch. Everyone likes ranch.

I've always wondered about that, Amy. Where did they get that name for a salad dressing?

Keep your mouth closed when you chew. No elbows on the table. Don't push your food around on your plate, eat it.

I like being part of a family. It's an army I can take and leave.

Gloucester has sons and Lear has daughters. What's Shakespeare telling us there? I resist the impulse to call the hotline, but I wonder. Kings only wanted sons. Maybe Lear was pissed about having daughters. Girls, what's the use of them?

There's a lot of use for 'em, said Knightley.

Gloucester doesn't do much of a job as a dad though. I don't think people back then thought about children the way we do. I'm not sure they even thought of their kids as children. So many of them died, they didn't even bother to name them until they felt the kid was going to live. Death raining down, death hanging around and picking his teeth, death going outside for a second to have a smoke but always coming back.

71

Amy and Hank have two daughters and a son, so they've got a fair allotment. Kids live from one year to another in America. They sit at a dining room table full of food. They aren't running through some village that's on fire, holding something in their hand and screaming this horrible wail. They aren't falling to the ground suddenly and not moving.

You know how we treat these people? We treat these people like Negroes. I ought to know, said Knightley.

Where you headed next, Tom?

East.

That's a big area.

Moments distend until they become larger than life. That's where Lear goes, into a moment. He's more than lost. He thinks he's still in time but he's outside of time. His appointment book is gone: 10 p.m.—heath party.

I guess I'll see Paula, so she can chew my ass—

The kids all look at me. So does Amy.

Sorry, slip of the tongue. Back to our casserole, gang. Knightley. I want to see Knightley, and I want to see Doreen.

Knightley, he's that African American buddy of yours, isn't he? Hank asks. The one you're always quoting, sort of a sage.

War is so stupid; how could anyone be a sage?

Amy's still looking at me. Are you and Doreen still an item?

An item? C'mon, that sounds like we appear in some society gossip column. Seen at the Copa last night were that ravaged but amiable vet and a certain veterinary technician.

The kids don't look at me. You listen to a lot when you are a kid that falls under the heading Stuff Adults Say. It's more word weather.

Don't quibble, Tom. Remember, no quibbling. Just answer, please. As your sister, I have an interest in your well-being.

I appreciate that. I wouldn't call us an item, though. We stay in something like touch. We don't talk about the range of our love lives.

The girls look up. Someone said the magic word.

Well, Amy says, maybe I'll meet her someday.

As if something regular could happen with me, as if I would show up sometime in a car trailing a few tin cans and "Just Married" scrawled on the rear window. I'd bounce up the front steps in a tuxedo, grinning like the Fourth of July.

Yeah, maybe you will. You know this casserole is better than I thought it was going to be. You must have aced home ec.

I didn't take home ec. That's slander.

Pray you now, forget and forgive.

The inconsequence of human talk, it's like our second oxygen. I'm good with that. It's not a play where everything's charged with the ions of discord. It's not a war. In the war, it was always weird calibrating our words. They had so little to do with anything but we needed them. That's why what they call "talk therapy" feels stupid to me, neither forgotten nor forgiven. What are we talking about when we talk about our shit?

I help clean up. Nice dishes, I say.

Amy starts laughing. Maybe you should have taken home ec, brother.

Maybe. Wandering around in the storm in an apron and waving a spatula. Good as anything.

God is my flak jacket.

Will you tell us a story, Uncle Tom? I will and I do. Once there was an old king who lost interest in being a king.

You've told us that one before, Uncle Tom.

Hang in there. This is a different version. In this version the king is elected.

Then he's not a king.

He's an elected king. It's different. Just listen. The king wins an election and decides he needs to undo what the last king has done. He has a choice. He can say the last king didn't know what he was doing or he can say that he knows better than the last king and can fix it up. Which do you think he chooses?

73

The kids whisper with one another. Kyle, the oldest, is the spokes-man. He says he knows better.

How did you guys know that?

They all giggle.

So the king tries to fix it and he makes things worse. Things are bad already but he makes things worse. It's sort of like when you have too much salt in the soup and then another cook comes in and throws in more salt.

Ugh, they say and make faces.

So things go downhill for the new king, but he keeps saying things are okay. Everyone around him says things are okay, too, though the people out in the countryside don't all say that.

This is getting boring, Kyle says.

Doesn't someone die? Katie, who is the one below Kyle, asks.

Lots of people die, I say.

Because there's a war? She asks.

Because there's a war.

Why are there wars? That's Miranda, the youngest. She tilts her head to the side the way a journalist does in a press conference.

So what happens? Kyle asks. Get to the point, Uncle Tom.

What happens is that the elected king gets unelected.

Unelected?

He starts thinking everyone is against him. All he is trying to do is make things right but everyone is against him. It's not fair. He starts to go a little crazy, walking around at night in the big house he lives in and talking to himself.

I like to talk to my dolls, Katie says.

The king loses it.

Loses it?

He starts to wander around outside and take his clothes off and yell at people. Some people try to help him and he starts to feel better but then—

Then what? They ask.

To be continued, I say.

They look at one another and then at me. That means later, right? Kyle asks.

That means later, I say. I try to smile but can't.

O you kind gods, cure this great breach.

But that's not a story, Kyle says. A story has an ending. A story has to have an ending, that's what makes it a story.

Amy's come into the living room. Uncle Tom looks tired, she says. You guys look a little tired, too.

The kids protest that they're not tired. They all jump up. They never get tired.

We didn't get to the end of the story about the king, Kyle says. He's perturbed.

I say I am tired.

I see myself with the king wandering around and trying to humor him and trying to convince myself that things will be okay. But what *things*? And what is *okay*? A gong is sounding inside me and it won't stop.

I'm going upstairs, I say.

When death is in the air, every step is laden. Death—car crashes, burst appendix, heart attack—is always in the air, but walking upstairs to the spare bedroom on the third floor can be trusted. It's automatic. Even though the moments are blind, one is securely linked to another. When Lear and Tom and the fool and Kent are out there getting their heads scrambled, death is in the air. There's a war coming.

Sound, trumpet! Blessed by extremity we sally forth.

Stormy weather, your certain steps may falter. Listen! The rain it raineth every day.

Telling the truth there, brother, said Knightley.

One minded like the weather, most unquietly. An anonymous gentleman in the play says that, someone without a name who pops up and then disappears. That's as scary as the people who have names, maybe more so.

I played a gentleman. I played a soldier. I got upstairs. It wasn't a big deal. It was a big deal, bigger than you'll ever know.

Tom's a-cold, I holler downstairs.

What's that? Amy says. I can't hear you.

I've got to use the phone, I say.

I ask Gwendolyn's sister if Gwendolyn is there. She asks who's calling. A friend of hers named Tom. I can feel she'd like to know more.

It's nice of you to call me, Tom, but I don't know what we can talk about. I'm going to be moving on soon. You could turn into a loose thread in my life. I don't want that.

It sounds like her voice is coming from outer space. I think of a song by the Rolling Stones: "It's so very lonely."

Just checking in, I say. I don't say, reporting for duty.

Look, Tom, you know how you talked about Shakespeare? It made me feel bad. I don't have a great education and when people talk about Shakespeare, I get nervous, like there's something huge out there I should know about and I don't and they do and they're better than me, even if the person is some kind of blown-away 'Nam guy.

I don't speak.

I'm sorry I said that but I had to. You know how I'm trying to be an actress. I'm trying to better myself. I'm trying to do something special. And I— she starts crying, little bursts and wheezes.

Then her sister's on the phone. Whoever the hell you are, you're making my sister—who is unstable to begin with—unhappy. She doesn't need another meathead in her life. Good bye.

I'm holding the receiver and listening to the dial tone. I wonder what the people in Lear's world would have made of all these weird sounds we take for granted: no engines, no electricity. If I were a director, I'd think first about the sounds those people heard. A storm was a storm back then, the to-and-fro wind, the pelting rain. Nature was the show.

I feel pretty lonely. It's not like I was cheating on Doreen. We aren't on the fidelity team. We're more like planets that orbit around one another and occasionally touch. We're both good with that. Not every love wants to go live in a house. Or so I tell myself.

I did the act of darkness with her. I was the beast.

Downstairs the kids must be playing some board game. They have those excited, deliberate voices kids get when they vanish into their imaginations.

Professor Cohen, this is Tom. Is the hotline open?

I have to go run some errands. Prescriptions, where would we be without chemical manna? I'm sure the pharmacist can wait ten minutes though. What's up? How are you doing?

I'm okay. I just had a not-so-great phone conversation but I'm calling about something I've been wondering a lot about since I first read the play, which was a long while ago, which is what makes a tragedy?

There's silence on the professor's end of the phone, then some throat clearing, then more silence.

Tragedy is what happens when great men fall. Great men for Shakespeare would be a king or someone like a king, a warrior like Othello or a noble like Macbeth or a prince like Hamlet or an emperor like Caesar. They all belong to the same group. There always is a martial element in the make-up of their world.

Martial?

War. Even in *Lear,* where we are focused on the king, there's a war in the background. So tragedy has something to do with the presence of war, as if war confirmed the stature of a king or maybe more because that's what kings did. They went on crusades and they fought other kings. But in any case, what made for tragedy was the stature of the king as a king and then who the king was as a human being. There always is a crack in that façade.

Silence.

Do you hear aught, sir, of a battle toward?

I'm listening, professor.

The crack comes from the disparity of the role, which requires some form of unremitting strength and often divine sanction, from the reality of human weakness, misjudgment, confusion, all the metaphysical maladies we are heir to. What is tragic is the great man's being caught in the human dilemma. The king is fallible. He has, in that sense, nowhere to turn. He is bound to err. Or Shakespeare sees him as bound to err. That dilemma moved Shakespeare deeply.

So an army private could not be tragic?

No. PFC Tom could not be tragic. Although they were far from magical creatures, there was a magic about kings. To show a king suffering was to take a vast step into something utterly unknown. There was no protection from being human.

I can see Lear at the end of the play. I can see the professor standing there scratching his head with the hand that isn't holding the phone receiver and thinking about how he has to go to the pharmacy. There's no way that life with its aimless lint is tragic. But it is.

He but usurped his life.

Sun came up today. Stop complaining, said Knightley.

You there, Tom?

The trick of that voice I do well remember.

I'm here. I mean I'm sort of here. I'm thinking but my head can't quite hold everything. I've got some mind leaks.

The hotline's shutting down for today. Take care, Tom.

I'm standing, admiring the sunlight coming through this big, dramatic window on the third-floor landing. Amy's house was built by some wealthy guy around 1900. They used to do things right.

And the girl coming toward me? Is that tragic? Or is death enough, all by itself? Or does war mock tragedy? Maybe I could have been a professor, answering unanswerable questions, chewing on words. Tom o' Scholar.

Are you done with the phone, Tom? Amy's one floor below me.

It's just a play, Amy is saying. She's older, so she can be oracular with me. The order of birth doesn't change; when we come to this world, etc.

I was just a soldier. You are just a wife and mother and sister and daughter. Cordelia was just honest. A war is just a war.

People shooting people, no big thing, happens among Negroes every day, said Knightley.

A math test is just a math test. Spilled milk is just spilled milk. A morning where you lie in bed and wonder what you are doing with your life is just that kind of morning, a wondering-about-your-life morning. There'll be others. Or there won't.

Don't exaggerate, Tom.

Don't employ, dear sister, the wiles of rhetoric that let us slip from day to day so that nothing ever fastens to us, so that we ride time without a further thought, so that we diminish our anguish in the service of convenience. When the Lear posse is out there in the storm or when the platoon is in the jungle or when the boat of fleeing Vietnamese is about to capsize, we don't say "just." We must honor extremities. Otherwise, we belittle our modest, daily stature.

Are you done, Tom?

There's the grand question. Tom seeks to keep himself alive. Tom seeks a greener field, another day, an explanation that makes perfect sense so that when the king walks out with his dead daughter in his arms, the universe does not dissolve but continues to oscillate to a frequency human beings cannot hear, but must trust, so that life going on is not a prison sentence—the heart's confinement.

Do you need a ride to the bus station?

I'd appreciate it.

I hug the children, shake hands with Hank, and think of calling Gwendolyn. On the way, in the car, Amy puts a hand over to me and squeezes my hand. She's here for me, she says. I nod. My hand squeezes back a little. I don't believe. What can I say? I don't believe.

79

I had it knocked out of me and trying doesn't do it. Trying is mostly bullshit. Trying is what sergeants make fun of: You tried, Tom, did you? What a good girl you are, you worthless asshole piece of shit.

Amy's still got my hand.

Two hands on the wheel, I say.

You sound like Dad, she says.

That leads us down the Dad alley. Both of us found him perplexing, though for different reasons. Amy wanted him to step up and I wanted him to step down. Women are looking for some signs of feeling. Men are looking for a little less male pressure. The pressure isn't feeling. It's—be a man. My dad wasn't a sergeant but there was that gene in him: straighten up, fly right, stand tall. When I got bounced for the girl's dorm room episode, he told me he wasn't surprised. I had a way of getting in my own way. Thanks, Dad. The worst part was the love that sat there between us like a boulder. We each pushed on it, I guess. Or we thought that was what love was—something in the way.

I don't tell Amy any of this sad male shit, though I suspect she's thought it more than once. She's had a father, has a husband and son.

> Fathers that wear rags
> Do make their children blind.

And that jacket you wear? Are you going to wear it until it falls apart? Or will you make another? What do you expect of life when you walk around telling the world that freedom is hell? Who, if I may ask, do you think you are? Amy pulls the car over to the curb. She leans her head over the steering wheel.

We fought in the name of freedom. War is hell, ergo freedom is hell. It's logic, a syllogism.

I don't know, Tom, and she picks her head up off the wheel. It's like men don't grow up or they grow up too much. They go someplace where no one can reach them. Or they do both at the same time.

There's a lot of bad noise inside of me, Amy.

What are you talking about?

Not guns and mortars, I'm talking about this other noise. It's in me. It's guys talking and it's speeches about what we were doing. It's silence because silence is awful, because it can't last and there's going to be hell to pay. It's the words that follow you around. That's what's in me. That's what my jacket is.

She's crying a little. I can feel my grimace. It's still Halloween for me.

Croak not, black angel; I have no food for thee.

I have the ridiculous feeling that things should work out. But they don't. Amy's sitting straight up. Her hands are gripping the wheel hard. She hasn't started the car. I remember you, Tom, when you were a little boy. You were sweet. You were a little out of it, too, the way Kyle can be out of it, just running along in his own head and not caring what the world thinks. My girls look over their shoulder at what the world is doing but Kyle doesn't do that. Neither do you, except that the world fell on top of you or exploded inside of you.

Evie says she's happy she's not a man.

We're all something. How's that for deep thinking? Amy smiles a bit, pulls a tissue from her pocketbook but doesn't do anything with it.

I'll be in touch, I say.

I don't doubt it, she says. Take care of that jacket. Take care of what's inside that jacket.

Make just report of unnatural and bemadding sorrow.

I will, I say.

In the bus station I can smell the unhappiness. I'm sure there are people who are eager to get on whatever bus, who are going to visit loved ones, as the expression goes, but there are more people who seem worn out, who shuffle across the unlovely linoleum, who cringe at the loudspeaker, who stare into space or pick at some forlorn sandwich they've pulled from a paper bag.

Ask me about the pathos of the human endeavor.

Do I exaggerate?

Pilgrims on the way to nowhere, they are keeping themselves going. There is a Dover for us and there is not a Dover. Some ultimate cloud hangs over our heads. You can feel it in the harsh fluorescent light, that relentless show of over-lit excitement. We can see! No blindness here! Meanwhile you can get your shoes shined by an elderly Negro man who wears suspenders and a Panama hat. What is the electoral month of November to him?

I represent the government. Put your hands up, said Knightley.

You can buy a magazine purveying excitement of some sort: politics, movie stars, health, sports, and up there on the far left corner, sex. I still have a fondness for *Playboy*. Sometimes it seemed that every inch of personal space the army allowed a guy would be plastered with pictures of the Promised Land. The magazine is in plastic these days, sometimes covered by a divider, as if to say, it's here but it would be better if it did not exist and your male prurience did not know about it.

Brass Balls, Hanging Heavy, All Night, Top Dog, those were helmet names. You hold on to what you have and you brag about it because one wound stuck in everyone's mind: take anything but don't take that.

I have a ticket to buy but I'm staring at a photo of some world leader. He's got a suit on and he's gesturing with his right hand. I should know who this is. Then again, I'm not going to run into him in any bus station. How are all The Important Things doing these days? I'd ask him. They seem to have lives of their own. I got a bit left behind. A decade chunks off like a glacier into the ocean. The "lost years" presumes there were some found ones.

> Welcome, then,
> Thou, o air, that I embrace!

Are you talking to yourself, mister? This is from a lady who's put a suitcase down beside me. She has on a big straw hat that I thought ladies didn't wear anymore. There are a couple of little red plastic balls attached to it. I think they're meant to be cherries. They have wire stems attached to them. I've got nothing against people talking to themselves, she says, don't get me wrong. You just don't want to be giving your secrets out in public. Then they wouldn't be secret. Get what I mean?

Yes, I say. The art of our necessities is strange.

What was that? She's one of those people who was a sheepherder in another life. She gathers strays.

She looks at my jacket. Were you there?

No, I say. It's an affectation.

A what? She says.

Where are you headed? I ask.

Wheeling, West Virginia.

Swell town, I say.

Not everyone feels that way but I do. When you get right down to it, there's no place that's as home as Wheeling. There's WWVA and the Jamboree. You know, son, you look a little like Merle Haggard.

Love cools, friendship rusts, brothers divide.
These dolorous fates roll and collide.

What's that you said, son? She tugs on an ear and inclines her head—the hard-of-hearing gesture.

Where did you get that hat?

Do you like it?

It's got a certain down-home flash. Wasn't there a gossip columnist who wore hats like that? Hedda Hopper—that was her name, she ruined a lot of people. She was a bitch.

Oh, I wouldn't know that.

There are probably some books about her. I bet the public library in Wheeling—

Nice talking with you. She picks up her suitcase.

Same here, I say, as she walks toward a far bench.

This is what I fought for, I say aloud but not very loud. I don't want to give anything away.

The bus holds that deep funk of thousands of perspiring bodies. I know that funk. The jungle is funky.

I throw my duffel on the seat next to me. There are a lot of people on the bus because it's going to wind up in New York City, though that seems like a week from now given all the scheduled stops.

I've thought of becoming a bus driver. I have a feeling for it. I like the idea of being quietly in charge, being more or less invisible to people. No one asks when someone gets off the bus, what did the driver look like?

What did the driver look like? What the fuck?

Regan and Goneril swear. Cordelia doesn't. Regan and Goneril get horny. Cordelia doesn't. Cordelia is too good for life. You never hear someone say that someone is too bad for life. Life seems to have infinite stretch in the badness department.

Our driver is a Negro man, in his fifties, graying at the temples and with that attitude of weary wisdom some Negroes have. You feel he's been through the storm. Now he's settling for the competence and semi-omnipotence of bus driving. Everyone should be seated. We're pulling out now. He has a dry, acute voice. He has studied dispassion.

Knightley used to tease all the white guys for even being in Vietnam. Everything working for you and your ass winds up here, you are some kind of natural fuck-up. You are a disgrace to the white race. War is for niggers to fight. Why else are there niggers? Didn't someone explain that to you?

There are still a couple of people looking for seats. I'm not the only one who has thrown a bag on the seat beside him. I slump toward the window, indicating I'm incommunicado. I'm bound for Parts Unknown, don't mess with me.

My wits begin to turn.

Son, do you mind?

It's a tall man in a black suit jacket who speaks to me. His hair is black and he has a lot of tonic on it. He also is holding a Bible.

No, sir, no problem, let me just move this bag that contains all my worldly possessions.

He gives me the eye but sits down.

Carry that around with you everywhere? I ask. I knew a couple of chaplains over there. Decent men, it wasn't their fault that what we were going through was unbearable. They tried to be upbeat in a serious way, the-Lord-is-with-us kind of thing, but they seemed bedraggled, as if they needed to make a direct call to God but couldn't get through. I knew some Bible-carriers, too, but steered clear of them. If they turned out to be safe, the guy next to them might not be. When one of them was killed, the rest of us thought the same thought, one more vaccine down the tubes.

The gods in the play are the old gods, pre-Jesus. You had to have a score card back then to keep track of them, sort of like when I was in junior high school and we had to learn all the people in the President's cabinet. I still can name the Postmaster General, which would be a pretty minor god.

I do, son. I'm an itinerant minister. I travel around this great world and preach God's word.

That's commendable, I say.

This world I do renounce.

I can wait. I've met preachers on the bus before. It's fertile territory for them, the rags and tags of the human race chewing Spearmint gum, drinking Coca-Cola, and mulling the essence of nothing. What does our locomotion mean?

You've read the Bible, son?

Many times, both the old and new parts, though the new part isn't so new anymore, is it? It's been awhile.

The work of Jesus is eternal, son. He smiles pleasantly. Good news.

Eternity's a big word, kind of overwhelming.

So should my thoughts be severed from my griefs.

It is a big word, you're right there. There are bigger words, though, like salvation and redemption. He sits back a bit, settling in. There's a lot to be said for having all the answers and being able to pull them out at your convenience. I can appreciate it. I can't say that my wandering has brought me anywhere. Doreen has told me I need to settle down, somewhere in her vicinity. We could get together when we wanted and be free when we wanted. I can't say, though, I've found a neighborhood that suits me. I keep seeing the houses explode.

When the words get big, I have a hard time keeping them in my little head. I smile pleasantly too, why not?

You're right there, son. It can get hard. What's your name, by the way? Tom.

Well, hello, Tom, my name's Jim, Jim Slayton. Pleased to meet you. Pleased to meet you, sir. My left hand shakes with his right.

I squat among the ruins of the living.
Listen to what fate has told me. Nothing!

Stormy weather, we've been having, I say, kind of late in the year for thunderstorms. I look into the autumnal gloaming. We're in the industrial wastelands outside of Chicago. Use up the earth: one thing we're good at. There are some weird flames coming out of very tall stacks. If you think it all makes sense, then it makes sense.

In this part of the world, it's not uncommon, he says.

You think God cares about the weather? I ask.

Come again, he says.

That's an expression I haven't heard for a long time. I had an aunt who used it. You'd say something to her and she'd say that as if you weren't speaking English. I guess the weather is just another variable for us, which I guess is fine. It's not boring.

No, it's not boring. He opens his Bible. May I read you something?

Actually, I'll pass on it, reverend. I got quite a bit in my head already, some of it, to tell the truth, is what you'd call heathenish. I don't want to get anymore mixed up than I already am.

He twists his head around to look more directly at me. We've been talking more to the air in front of us than to one another.

Do you believe you have a soul, son?

That's a big question for some strangers who have been talking for a few minutes on a bus. I think there's an interstate commerce act about asking that question but what I believe is that I had a soul but I lost it.

Lost it? He looks even more directly at me. I expect him to wipe his eyes as if to be sure he's seeing what he's seeing.

Some prodigy lurks here, some phantasm,
Some spirit of the night that bodes no man well.

I was a kid once, running around and yelling and climbing trees and riding a bicycle. I was a young man once, who felt how urgent each day was and who, you'll pardon the expression, wanted to get laid. But I read books and tried to think about what was in them, maybe the way you think about the Bible, but maybe not. And then I was a soldier, which I fell into and let it carry me along. And then I was riding buses talking to people, reverends, for instance, and trying to explain myself and not doing a particularly good job of it. I can feel something inside of me starting to crack.

Five fiends have been in poor Tom at once.

The reverend makes a kind of harrumph sound. He's not an unkind man. I've met a few who were unkind, who felt they had an obligation to get in your face until there was no room left between them and you and you couldn't breathe for the closeness of it, for the pressure of their missionary truth.

Jesus is smart, said Knightley. He stays in a church, not some jungle.

I see, he says.

You probably don't. I don't say that out of disrespect. I say that because I can't see and I'm the one who's living it. Everyone has their patter but if you lose the patter, if you lose the thread, and I don't care if it's God or baseball or politics, then you wind up watching everybody including yourself making signs more than talking. Signs like "Don't Walk Here" or "Look Out."

Jesus can speak to you, son. I have met many confused souls—

Remember, I lost mine. That's important. When you lose it, you don't get it back.

Mercy, the forgiveness that God—

Those are more words, reverend. I don't want to get steamed up so we better drop this.

I can see the girl moving toward me. There I am. I'm afraid of a girl. Then she falls down, not like in some slow-motion movie, but fast, the life gone out of her so she's nothing more than the weight of a body.

I cannot daub it further. So bless thee, master.

That's a Vietnam jacket you're wearing, he says.

It is.

I can understand. I've counseled a few men. God's word is for everyone. There's that firm, hopeful note in his voice. He can reel this one in.

I got back to a different place, reverend. It's not like I want to stay there but I got back to where people don't get saved, they only live and die. Not to be brusque, but that's all the sermonizing for today. I turn my head to the window and the night and the passing cars.

He makes a throaty sound, some words caught in his mouth that don't get out.

O gods! Tom exclaims because there isn't just one. There's a bunch of them looking down on us and wandering through the air and living in trees. I need to ask the professor about that. I need some sleep. Too many spirits are loose.

Fort Wayne, the bus driver announces. I've just woken. The reverend's gone but the bus is still full. Fort Wayne, he repeats. We've slowed down and must be near the bus station. I don't know anyone in Fort Wayne. I've never been there. I grab my duffel and when the door opens, I'm out of it.

Maybe I could live here. Everyone lives in some particular place, unless you're a migrant. Those are the terms of residing on earth. Maybe Fort Wayne could do it for me. More likely, I just couldn't be on that bus anymore. The vagaries of conversation have been known to spook me. Tom's liable to spooking. He can talk about himself in third-person as if he's someone else because he is. He's left himself behind, which is what I meant when I told the reverend about losing my soul.

I need to take a long walk so I store my duffel in a locker in the bus station. It's raining but I've got a poncho—army surplus for army surplus.

I feel terrible, like the wind and the rain, like the deep that broods upon the earth is right on top of me, excavating the soul that I told the preacher I lost. Be kind, Tom. He can't help it if he has the answers. He's lost track, though, of how big the questions can get. He thinks everything has been resolved. The story is over but it isn't.

I've gotten rained on before. Over there, the rain is serious, torrents of it. You feel you don't have a body anymore. You feel that you are going to dissolve and join the rain. And some of us did.

What does the weatherman say? Fucked again, that's what he says, said Knightley.

So I walk. I'm not here to reconnoiter. I'm not doing a report. There are houses and stores and gas stations and churches, don't forget the churches. A lot of people live here, more or less contentedly. This is home for many and I can look at the dark houses and think about the people inside them and how each one of them has some story to tell him or herself that keeps the storm outside at bay.

Some don't have that story but I don't see them on the streets tonight. They have better things to do than aimlessly wander. I don't have time to kill. I have time to fill. I can hear the rain and the wind in the trees. I can remember how, as a boy, they seemed like voices speaking to me.

What is your study?

How to prevent the fiend, and to kill vermin.

Stop! I shout. I think I shout, maybe it's in my head. No, I shout, stop! She doesn't. She keeps heading toward me. She's saying something. Why am I somewhere where I don't even know the language of the people that I'm with? Stop!

Every word that's been said about the war comes over me, more words than could ever be counted, a blizzard, a flood, but those are natural things and the words that get said aren't natural. They come out of human heads. They're full of that bad assurance that comes out of human heads: *I know what I'm talking about.* Every discussion, every speech, every newscast, every press conference, every article in every paper, every debate, every lecture, every phone call, all snowballing until it lands on some kid with a rifle who learns to speak his own sort of knowledge, which can be summed up by the word *shit.* And then more words to justify the first words, to make up, to explain, to console.

I stop in the middle of a block of little houses built probably after WWII for returning vets in search of the Good Normal Life. Some of the yards have fences, chain link, but a few with wooden pickets. Keep it out and keep it in, each to his propertied own. It's still raining, maybe a little harder, though I've lost track. My feet are soaked but the rest of me is reasonably dry. I feel weary, like I want to lie down right here on the sidewalk.

I keep walking. Blocks devour blocks, lives devour lives.

Yours in the ranks of death.

The wind seems to have picked up. I'm alone on the earth in a storm. I'm not the last man, so much as I'm the only man. I wish I had a task but then I don't wish that. I've had it with tasks. I wish I could float like the leaves coming off the trees. That's what I am doing, though. I don't have to wish. I'm with the wind and the rain. I'm an element.

This night the sky comes near to speech but halts.

I hear beside me the squish of tires on the wet asphalt, a car slowing to a stop. Hey, buddy, what you up to? The voice is friendly enough, but practiced, a voice that has a job. Kind of a messy night to be taking a walk. A policeman is leaning toward the open window on the passenger side. You lost?

No more than I usually am.

That doesn't answer my question. He raises the window some to keep out the lashing rain.

I like weather. I like being out in weather. Makes you know you're alive.

Well, that's nice but people in Fort Wayne get nervous when someone's walking around in the middle of the night. They think that person might have some bad thoughts on his mind.

Why would anyone want to break into one of these melancholy houses?

Apparently the cop has never considered that question. He clears his throat, an official remember-I'm-in-charge action.

You could get sick out here tonight. Maybe you should think about getting in this car with me and letting me take you to some motel where you can dry your bones. You have any money? You homeless, broke?

Thou wert better in a grave than to answer with thy uncovered body this extremity of the skies.

I appreciate your kindness, officer, but I want out of houses. That's why I'm walking. I had too much of houses. I was in a house and I listened to records and watched TV and hid *Playboy* under my bed and ate hamburgers and what happened to me? I became another badly working part in a bad machine. I became a motto in another forgettable speech. I wave my arms to gesture — a benediction and dismissal.

He nods in a show of patience. My interest in you, he says, holds a thin edge. The law is what an officer construes it to be.

You weren't an MP once upon a time, were you?

I was.

But not in 'Nam?

No, not in 'Nam. I'm younger. I missed all the fun.

I thought so.

And you had something to do with it?

Something.

You're getting awful wet standing there.

I am. It's thrilling. Goodnight, officer. And off into the night I walk as he drives off, his tires bequeathing a dense kiss to the unlovely street. He could have run me in for vagrancy or whatever else—confused threat to society, aging delinquent, moral cipher, sober and disorderly. I thank him for keeping the peace.

Fellow feeling among strangers is the crucial quotient. Any family can go to hell. You don't have to have daughters like Regan and Goneril. Any kids will do; any parents. You can't judge anything by what families do, but strangers, that's another story. Strangers can be alive to each other. Family members have their practiced knowledge: he hath ever but slenderly known himself. She's right, too. Lear's bad girls were bad but they weren't stupid. They had their reasons.

How tiresome we become to one another.

I keep walking. I don't expect a phantom of forgiveness to emerge out of the rain that's started, at last, to let up. I'm here, not there. I'm clear about that. It's that I need to get dead tired. When I do, when I feel the living ache subside, I'm near a strip of fast food joints and auto repair shops—brakes, transmissions, bodywork—and a motel with a light on. I get a room—the night clerk can't be more than eighteen and is reading a paperback novel with a literary cover, no hand guns or half-naked women—and take a hot shower and lie down on a bed that speaks for the penury of the whole economizing universe: sparse blanket, worn sheets, thin mattress. I could sleep on the floor but what passes for the carpet is not appetizing. A hovel would be much better. Maybe that's what I'm looking for—a hovel to call my own, not a house, but something light, something the liberating forces can torch without a second thought because it barely seems to be there.

Fire it up.

Is there any morning in *King Lear*? Is the whole thing at night? I'm on the hotline with the professor. I'm lying on the bereft bed with a Styrofoam cup of bad coffee in my other hand. Is there any sun in the play? The professor reminds me how the sun and moon, according to Gloucester, have been "late" eclipsed and how the world is going to hell, the way the world is always going to hell—mutiny, treason, discord, you name it, every damn trouble. Edmund makes fun of him, his father acting like someone who reads the astrology column in the daily paper and takes it seriously. Don't join the army today if you're a Gemini; Aquarians, good day to get a haircut; Leos, see a vocational counselor about attending fool school.

Then the professor quotes how Lear swears by the "sacred radiance of the sun." Lear doesn't stop there, though. After all, if we all got up and said, "Well, the sun's up, everything's okay—" that would be too simple. The sun is "sacred," which is nice because it shows some strong feeling, but tough because whatever is sacred is distant and untouchable. It's a special category, like some girl you had eyes for in high school but never could imagine asking out.

The professor goes on about "the mysteries of Hecate and the night" and how that's where the play resides. The sun is a ploy. There has to be the sun for anything to happen, but what's exciting, what gives life its rough grain, is night, which is ruled by a witch. Witch-fear is night-fear and woman-fear because night is an unbounded woman, not tied to the rules of men and their sun-kings. When Lear divvies up his kingdom, it may be daytime but it's really nighttime, blindness ruling, darker purpose.

Pleasant dreams, said Knightley.

I tell the professor about my room in the motel and the coffee that comes from some bag whose contents you pour into a little machine. It's a convenience, I say. I hear my voice—flat and bitter.

No one, Tom, makes you drink that stuff. You act as though the universe is complicit with your every action. You act as though fate is bearing down on you every second.

Is there time-out? I ask.

There's only so much dire residue, he says.

For awhile we're both silent then he says he has to go.

I say bye. He hangs up. I stare at the receiver. I should have kept talking. I should have asked him about his health. I should give up on regret. I should toss this foul brew down the drain.

King Lear—a king—didn't know what futility was. You can't be human—someone who puts his or her head down on the bar counter and cries—if you don't know that. I think that's one thing Cordelia is trying to show him, how to be more and less than a role, not the powerful, royal "we." *Be a person, be my father,* she's saying to him. She trusted sincerity. She was too trusting; she died for it, but the other side is inhuman like her sisters. They died, too. Where, oh where, does that leave me?

I hear this pissed-off, electronic sound. Hello, Tom, you need to put the receiver down. I chuck the coffee. I see a stain in the sink that probably comes from many cups of bad coffee. I make the bed even though it's going to be unmade.

Sometimes, like now in this room, I wish I could talk to the girl. I wish I could find out who she was. I wish I could hear her say anything; even that she hated me; even that she wished I was dead instead of her.

You're weak, Tom. You hide behind words. You admire your agony.

I keep meaning to learn their language.

I cannot heave my heart into my mouth.

Doreen, I wobble into the receiver, it's me.

I know your voice, dodo sweetheart. Where in this big world are you?

Fort Wayne, Indiana, in a motel.

That sounds right. Probably a pretty depressing place that gives you that large fraction of misery you tend to crave. Is that right, lover boy?

Don't start in, Doreen.

Start in? I don't hear from you for weeks that become months and I'm starting in? I should hang up now.

Don't do that. Please.

I don't just exist in your head, Tom. I'm a woman and though plenty of times I don't want to have feelings for you, I do. And you take advantage of that. Do you understand? You take advantage of that. You're not the only man on my plate, we both know that, but that doesn't mean you can act as though I don't care, when I do care. If you let me, I could care even more.

She starts crying. It's a sudden trigger but there it is.

I join in.

Cadent tears fret channels.

> Old fond eyes,
> Beweep this cause again I'll pluck ye out.

I didn't mean to start in on you, Tom, she says through sniffles and sobs. I've missed you. I don't know what you tell yourself but I've missed you. Do you get that?

I nod to the receiver. Yes, I moan.

> I want to feel.
> I don't want to feel.
> I want to feel.
> I don't want to feel.

So, what are you going to do about it? You're coming here, right? And maybe you're going to take part in the parade for the Wall. It's not like I would say that would be nice because I know how you feel, but it's going to happen and it might help you to be with all those others. They're sort of like brothers, right?

I've avoided being part of any larger group since I was a member of a larger group. When my dad took me to the VFW in our town there were those skeptical looks from the older guys, the Korean War and WWII guys, about what kind of war I'd been in—which meant a losing war, an un-clear-cut war, a weird war. One evening was enough.

Well—

I know. I'm pushing you. Someone breathes on you and they're pushing you.

Hey.

Hey, what? Hey to the time in front of us not the time behind us. Hey to the sun coming up in the morning. Hey to my being a woman and your being a man.

I don't know about the parade. I've read about the Wall, though.

You're on earth, that's great. A woman designed it, not some general. You know that, right?

I do. Some woman who didn't die at the end of the play, some woman who wasn't played for a bitch, shot or raped, her body tossed into a ditch. Bye-bye mama-san. No headline for you.

You there, Tom?

I'm here and I'll be there. Love you.

I appreciate the sentiment, honey, but I need to see the money. Bye, dodo.

I spend too much time staring at phone receivers. Along the way, I lost my briskness.

We'll set thee to school with an ant.

The motel's morning clerk is a hearty guy with a formidable gut. He calls a cab to get me to the bus station and talks about how Fort Wayne is "on the way up." There's a new this and a new that.

Sometimes I feel that America needs to take a rest, I say. You know like half-time.

He smiles funny at me. Your cab should be here any minute, he says, and ducks into a room behind the front desk.

> The land of Disney is red, white and true.
> Mickey and Donald went to war for you.

The cabbie, an older guy who smells like wet dog, keeps changing the radio station like he wants to hear ads not music but doesn't say a word. After I get my duffel and after a mild hassle about my ticket, because I got off the bus but after I explain and gesticulate that I had an emergency, I'm five rows back on the driver's side beside an older woman who's knitting something pink.

How are you today, son?

I have a lot of unresolved grief about shooting a girl in a war, along with self-hatred, but otherwise I'm fair to middling, trying to put my life together, and a bunch of other clichés. Thanks for asking. And I'm older than you may think.

Well, I'm Sally Johnson—my friends call me Johnny, that's funny isn't it, a boy's name—and my heart goes out to you, son. She stops her knitting and looks at me. That's a nice jacket you have there.

Thanks.

And what war was it? She asks. Her voice is peaceful and almost speculative.

Vietnam.

I didn't pay that war much attention. I know it was a big deal but I don't follow the news much. I'll tell you one thing, though. Wendell Wilkie was a good-looking man.

Wendell Wilkie, huh?

You get as old as I am and it seems as if you've seen it all. She sighs.

I feel like that too, I say.

War's a hard thing, she says. Young boys dying. She keeps on knitting.

What's that you're knitting? I ask.

It's going to be a sweater for my granddaughter Carolyn. That's where I'm headed, to Lima, Ohio, where she lives with her mom Carrie and her dad Joe. She chuckles. They're quite the pair Carrie and Joe, what you'd call live wires.

I make a humming, telegraphic sound. I, too, wish I could graze in the fields of regularity. Time would milk me each day. I'd give forth a pail's worth of self-satisfaction. The seasons would pass the way they were intended to pass. I'd be almost Biblical—Tom the Revelator. I exhale hard.

You got a cough there, son? I've got some cough drops in my purse. Johnny puts her knitting down, pulls up a voluminous bag from the bus floor and begins to paw through it.

It comes back to me how much I used to like to suck on cough drops when I was a boy. They probably were pure sugar. Somehow I felt I was doing something good for myself. I take one from Johnny and begin to suck.

I guess it's too bad we have to have these wars, she says. The Germans were terrible people. Imagine someone being like Hitler. A little termite, that's what my late husband called him. She looks down at the pink whatever it is she's knitting. She shakes her white head of little permed curls.

> He that will think to live till he be old,
> Give me some help.

Well, you keep knitting there, Johnny. I'm going to take a snooze. I didn't get much sleep last night.

Tossing and turning, son?

Yeah, a lot of tossing and turning.

Her neat little mouth makes a neat little smile. Sympathy goes forth a little ways then bows to the non-existent audience.

I close my eyes but the scenario remains: everyone is employed gainfully in the sense-making capacity while I'm standing in the wings waving a battered copy of a battering play. I see myself sitting in some old theater from the last century and watching actors dressed up in their robes and finery declaiming and gesticulating. Their voices reach the heavens. There still were heavens to reach. I fall asleep.

It's Lima, I hear Johnny say.

Ah, Lima, Ohio! Home of, famous for, birthplace of, settlers first, coming soon, in this location, the oldest living, state champions: every unspecial place is special. You might as well love America because it doesn't know any better. It's all good, even the bad is good. Love Us, Love Our Wars.

Don't be bitter, Tom.

Why not?

You take care of yourself, son. Don't take any wooden nickels. Johnny winks at me. I wonder what I was dreaming about when Lima appeared. I've had the nightmares on the bus: private hell in a public space.

I look out the window at what passes for a bus station. One of the chaplains I talked about said to me one morning when we were admiring some landscape that hadn't been blown up or defoliated that God didn't cut corners when He made the earth. He left it to the human race to cut corners, though the chaplain never would have said that.

Johnny gives me a jolly wave as she steps down from the bus. She's done her part. She's got some knitting to show for it, too. Maybe you need a hobby, Tom, something to take your mind off your troubles. Maybe I could rig up a little theater in one of my sisters' cellars and make figures out of wood and do *King Lear* to my heart's sad content. As my ideas go, it's not the worst one. Maybe, to start with, I need my own cellar, though owning anything big bothers me. Me and my duffel, me and my shadow, me and my memory: trying to lift my insubstantial weight.

> But thou dost breathe
> Hast heavy substance.

No one gets on in Lima, but Dayton is full of people heading east. A number of them eye the seat beside me but head down the aisle in search of more amenable pastures. Let poor voke pass. I have been known to be ill-disposed. Fragments inside me trying to get out.

Anyone claim this seat? It's a teenage girl, maybe around sixteen. She's clutching a small backpack to her chest. Her voice is breathy, maybe a little scared.

Claim? What script is this?

I wave a welcoming hand and she sits down, but rigidly, holding onto the backpack for, what my mother habitually called, "dear life."

"To Whomever It May Concern (and I hope it concerns someone): I am writing to tell you that I am not dead yet," said Knightley (dictating to Tom).

Headed all the way through? I ask.

She turns her head. She wasn't expecting a question. Maybe that's why she sat here, thinking I was the silent type.

To Wheeling, she says. I have a cousin there I'm going to visit. But my parents don't know I'm going so I'm sort of running away. She lets go of the backpack enough to start twirling a piece of her long dark hair. She really is a cousin. It's not like when you tell the guidance counselor that a friend of yours is pregnant which means that you're pregnant. Know what I mean? She stops the twirling and looks at me. Brown eyes flecked with green.

She has a widow's peak, too, that little V of hair at the top of her forehead.

I know what you mean. I need to say something more. She's looking at me to say something. It's best, I say, if we own what we say.

What crap.

She wants more than platitudes but Edgar tends to platitude, doesn't he? When he finally tells his father who he is, his father dies. Maybe he should have kept quiet. The weight of this sad time we must obey, he says at the end. No one has obeyed much of anything throughout the whole play, everyone keeps challenging everything, and Edgar preaches obedience. He barely has anyone to speak to. Practically everyone's dead. There's been a war in the background and a war in the foreground, the War of the Family, the enmity compounded of familiar strife. Maybe at the end he's numb, a human ruin. Maybe it's amazing he can talk at all.

I don't get along at home, she says. It's not one big thing but a lot of little things: hassles, trying to keep me from growing up, always telling me what to do, and what to watch out for. I guess they mean well but I need some time out. She puts the backpack, which has been sitting in her lap, onto the bus floor and pulls out a book: *The Catcher in the Rye*. She shows me the book and opens it and then looks at me and all of a sudden she's crying; real loud and almost hysterical, and other people on the bus start craning their necks and then she leans her head into my side so the sound is lessened but she's still crying.

I guess I attract it, a walking soap opera. All the tears held back in the play fall on me.

Is something wrong? A woman behind us asks.

There usually is when people cry, I say.

The woman snorts a fuck-you-Jack snort.

Did you ever? Another woman says.

The girl stops heaving—this all doesn't take long, but feels like those war moments when time got lost, when the moments were much bigger than you. It was like drowning.

What time is it? It's the wrong time. That's what time it is, said Knightley.

She raises her head, wipes at her nose with the cuff of her jacket then sweeps her hair back.

Sorry, she says.

I—

It's all worse than I said. You knew that, right?

I—

But I don't want you to help me, you understand? I didn't sit down next to you so you could help me. I have to do things for myself. Getting away is something I'm doing for myself. She takes another wipe with her cuff. I'm so embarrassed, making a scene like that, like I'm a little crybaby or something.

It'd be a better world if more people cried in public. There's too much business and not enough crying.

Be your tears wet?

You're good with crying? I mean do you cry? You've got that jacket on and you cry?

Too much and not enough.

That's like something Holden might say. Did you read this when you were my age? But—and another cuff wipe to her nose—what's the book you've got there? It looks pretty beat-up.

King Lear. I like beat-up books. It's like love, the kind where you can't let go.

I've been in love twice. It sucks. I know who Shakespeare is. I read *Julius Caesar* last year. I can't say I was crazy about it. It didn't have much to do with me living in Dayton.

King Lear doesn't just have something to do with me. It is me.

What's that you're saying?

> For many miles about
> There's scarce a bush.

I got a reason. It's a rifle, said Knightley.

Sometimes, there's no space between you and the book. Maybe *The Catcher* is a little like that for you.

A little. Holden's a guy so there's that. He sort of lays it on too thick, the way guys lay it on too thick. He sees shit, though. She puts her hand over her mouth. Whoops, I said a swear.

I don't know what help I could give you anyway. I look down at *Lear,* which is the conflated text. I like that word. You don't see it much. Rhymes with elated, misstated, prated. The words are always there in the background chiming away, the supporting cast.

You already have helped, Mister—

Tom, Mister Tom.

Maybe you'll tell me about the play.

People wander around. People do bad things to other people. People suffer. No one really knows what's happening but everyone keeps talking. Sometimes the talk is like lightning in the night. Sometimes it's silly. Sometimes it's mean, very mean. Sometimes you have to put the book down, or if you were watching the play you'd have to close your eyes. Things go really wrong.

That seems kind of chicken, to close your eyes.

Maybe, but it would be like if you told me the worst thing and then something happened to you that was even worse.

Even worse?

> I am only sorry
> He had no other deathsman.

We should let this stuff go. It's been good to meet you. Your name is?

Lisa, she declares in a forthright, front-of-the-stage voice. You're right. I have to think about what I'm going to do next. I mean after I talk to my cousin.

Cordelia, what comes into my head again is Cordelia. How old was she? Did she have a widow's peak? I've told Doreen about Cordelia. She's read the play more than once but it's more than reading the play. There's this sense of how Cordelia is telling us something but it's not just in her words. It's her being. The way the war is in my being, there's something in her being. I can call it "goodness" but it's not the right word. It has to do with her being alive and being charged with love. And it's a charge, like a command, but it's natural, too, like a flower or a horse, but not sentimental, true-hearted.

I look over at Lisa who's writing in what looks like a diary.

Cordelia has to die. That's the crux. Is her love impossible? Is that why she has to die? Or maybe she's practical and honest, like when she talks about how she is going to love her husband not only her father. But why does she have to die then? Is it like when everything starts to go to hell so there's no other place to wind up but hell? You can't expect to pull sunshine out of hell.

Myself could else outfrown false Fortune's frown.

You got your share of worrisome thoughts there, Tom. Not doing you much good, though, said Knightley. Rocket's coming when it's coming.

Take heed, this blunted world's a heedless place.

Lisa looks up from her writing. It's a journal. I've been keeping it since I was twelve. It's the one thing I have that's mine. But I'm wondering, Mister Tom, where are you headed?

DC. I'm going to see a girlfriend, spend time with one of my sisters, check out an old buddy, maybe do a little sight-seeing, take in a few memorials.

Sort of a vacation? Or are you sort of always on vacation?

Well, no, actually—

Lisa waves a hand that still has her pen in it. So, you probably figured out I'm on this bus because my parents are both drunks. Not just one of them but both of them. My dad works in an office and comes home and drinks, one after another so he's blotto by nine o'clock. My mom's at it all day, so she's semi-coherent when my dad comes home, and they act as though we're a family, and then she's out of it by nine o'clock, too, and I guess that's when I come to life. I guess I'm a night person who has to go to school all day and raise her hand and gossip about which boy you'd like to bone you and where did you get those shoes. She points to the journal. I've filled a bunch of these things.

Well—

Don't feel sorry for me, Mister Tom. I've got life in front of me, right? That's what I tell myself. I've got some nicks in me but that's okay.

You're wise, Lisa, beyond your years. You could be in this play, and I point to the book. There's a sort of wisdom here. Not the spume of rhetoric or drizzling wit or self-satisfied shibboleths, but intelligence that's born from the travails of experience: confusion, betrayal, pride.

You talk a little funny, Mister Tom. Do you know that? Where do you come from?

> I'll look no more
> Lest my brain turn, and the deficient sight
> Topple down headlong.

Uncle Sam Land, it's due west of Dover.

Lisa ducks her head. I've got to write more. Bye now.

I met this strange guy in a funny jacket on the bus.

Ohio passes by in that wan November light that suits Ohio.

Lisa looks up. Did you see people get killed? She looks steadily at me but with a child's look. She might as well be asking if I have an apple in my pocket.

I did. It's only two little words but they sound husky. The feeling comes on like that.

And did you kill people?

A lot of people are shooting all at once. It can be hard to tell. It can be impossible to tell. You're so out of your mind while trying to stay in your mind that you aren't the world's most reliable observer. It's not like hit-the-balloon with a bb gun at the county fair.

Do I see the girl coming toward me? I see the girl.

I'm sorry, Mister Tom. I'm really sorry. Now her voice has cracks in it. Then she reaches a hand out and touches my hand.

I'm sorry too, I say.

Here is a pocketful of *sorry*. Hold out thy hands. Accept this nothing.

More Ohio and then Wheeling and Lisa is getting up and I do, too. Time to stretch my bus-bound legs. We shake hands in the station. There's no one there to meet her, but she goes to a phone and makes a call while I try not to hover nearby but I keep an eye out, as if I could do something for her. She talks some and then hangs up and gives me a little wave and she's out the door.

Holden lives.

No one told Shakespeare these stories on a bus. He read them in this or that book and then made a lot up. It's nothing against my story, or Lisa's story, or the guy in front of me at the station's ancient newsstand who's buying the local paper and a PayDay candy bar. It's that there are larger stories and he told them. Our stories are small and they press in on us.

You cross off the days behind you, not the days before you. Doing this, being here, you need the right arithmetic, said Knightley.

I buy a PayDay too, and then call up Paula.

It's—

I know my brother's voice. Where are you?

Paula is smart. She tries to make life smart, too.

On the heath, I say. The weather's sunshine and rain.

Don't start in with the play, Tom. Let's just be in America now. Maybe you're in Cumberland, Maryland.

Wheeling, West Virginia.

I wasn't too far off. And you are arriving when?

I don't know, I'd guess around six.

There are these things called "schedules." Buses run on them.

Six, I say. It seems a truthful number.

I'll see you then, she says. I'm looking forward to catching up. Bye.

She's not one to spout the word "love." When we were growing up, she was the explainer in the family. It's a big job. It's not that she's cold. It's that she has a hard time waiting for the world to catch up with her.

I walk up and down the sidewalk outside the station while I eat my candy bar. I think of Lisa knocking on some door and wondering if the door will open. I think of Paula shaking her head after she puts the receiver down. I think of Doreen and then Knightley. I don't know where Knightley lives. The address I have, which is who knows how many years old, is where his mother lives. Maybe he lives there. A guy goes to the other side of the world to fight a war and winds up living with his mother.

I deposit the candy wrapper in a trash bin on whose side is written DON'T LITTER.

My arm extends this far but no further. My steps go this far—to the verge—but no further.

 Come, sit thou here, most learnèd justice.

And what about those on that other side of the world, who were there before we came? What about the people we were there to help, and to whom we never really spoke; whose country we inhabited as we chased the enemy, who also were people who were there before us? How could we transport one reality and set it down in another so that there was no reality, but a bizarreness in which there was no up or down, right or wrong, day or night? Where did we get off doing that?

American know-how, American not-know-how, everything greased by machines and money, headed everywhere in a hurry, capable of going anywhere and wanting to make them into us, even as we said we weren't interested in making them into us. No sirree, no way, Jack, let them be Vietnam (often pronounced as two syllables, as in Veet-Nam, long *e* and wrenched, nasal *a*), just let it be our democratic Vietnam: Dennis the Menace, Bob Hope, President Nixon, Dallas Cowboys; all the tense, jostled, messianic joy of the last best hope. Let us do it, whatever it is! We can win, joke, do good, and kill at the same time! Welcome to the wheel of fire!

Did the president call while I was taking a dump? asked Knightley.

I need another candy bar, probably a Coke too, to further ruin my insides.

Eastbound bus leaving in five minutes. I look around for Lisa to appear. I touch my face. Have I been talking to myself again? I lack a proper stage. I wait until the last thirty seconds but she's gone into her beckoning life.

My copy of *King Lear* has reserved my seat for me. No sitting or lying down where tragedy lurks. Could be harmful to your soul's health, cause distressing dreams, and generally make you doubt the purposeful drift of your fibrous existence. Yes, madam or mister, your life is a miracle, but a miracle that proceeds from day to day is no longer a miracle but rather a spectacle and then, after many days, no longer that, but a shapeless, colorless rag that you wear without a second thought because it is yours—your life, the once ravishing whole diminished to a possessive pronoun.

No one sits beside me. There's enough room on this bus for everyone to have an area to him or herself. No need to accommodate one's self to some other self, however briefly or formally. Pleasantly, the vast, passing spaces of the continent echo inside us, a sort of metaphysical hum, long-distance bus travel being a relatively cheap tranquillizer.

I finish my PayDay. Salted peanuts and caramel, you can't beat it. Then I start at the beginning. I thought the king had more affected the Duke of Albany than Cornwall.

Businessmen commenting on another businessman, no women in sight, and nothing actual, nothing but a thought on the part of Kent; not a tree or a pear or a kiss, but a thought that's bound to make more thoughts because that's what thoughts do; they're like the amoebas they taught us about in high school, proliferating at blinding speed. Heady. And there's the specter of favoritism: if someone wins, someone loses; if someone is raised up, someone is cast down. It sounds Biblical but we know what's bound to happen. Division creates division; the equal parts are never equal.

I down my Coke. My stomach gurgles in protest.

I see the dukes and the king as statesmen, secretaries of state and advisors, the guys who move the pawns around on the big board, the guys who are a galaxy away from the real pawns with their uniforms and dog tags and thirty-second haircuts. They are the guys who show up and take a quick look and decide everything is okay because for them it is okay because they're not witnessing a war. They're witnessing their own thoughts. They live back home, safe in their offices with their thoughts.

But the guys in Shakespeare aren't safe, are they? They're in for some serious hell. Some of them are going to buy it. Those walls of words that our guys have aren't there for them.

Would you turn that noise down? Someone who's two seats behind me is asking someone three seats behind me. The kid has headphones on but there's some leakage, a sort of metal thud I can hear where I am, as if Odin had a drum kit. You could scream that the apocalypse is coming in five minutes and the kid wouldn't hear you.

The guy who has made the request stands up and mimes taking off the headphones. I've turned around to watch because I like theater. And it's funny, isn't it, how after Kent and Gloucester are done talking about kingdom-dividing, Gloucester starts talking about sex. What could be more natural? I bet Nixon and his henchmen did it all the time: here's Vietnam and here's a smutty joke. Can you tell the difference?

The kid with the headphones, who is draftable age, gangly, big Adam's apple, takes off the headphones but the music is still roaring. AC/DC, he announces. He smiles, part-truculent and part-goofy.

Look, says the other guy, who's older but not by a whole lot, maybe his late twenties, I have papers to go through and he waves a few manila folders with blue tabs on them. Please turn it down.

Highway to Hell, the kid says and looks around the bus as if searching for other AC/DC fans.

I don't care what it is, just turn it down.

Okay, the kid says. I can do that. And he turns the volume down on his little machine. Highway to Hell, he says one more time and puts the headphones back on. His smile is gone. He's a serious kid. His song matters.

Thanks, the older guy says, and sits back down to resume his share of America's never-ending work.

A lady further back says that she never heard of that song. She says she's a Liberace fan. A musical discussion ensues.

I cannot conceive you, says Kent. The puns are relentless. I tried to explain it more than once to Knightley who had more verbal sense than me, who could have been some kind of professor, but thought it was bullshit. Hard life takes the play out of you.

I could use another PayDay. I could use Doreen's head on my shoulder. I could use sitting in Knightley's kitchen, or his mother's kitchen, and drinking a cup of coffee, and not reminiscing, but being in whatever present moment we could fashion for ourselves. I could use a headphone set myself. I keep meaning to make up a list of things I could use.

I turn to the end of the play. Enter Lear, with Cordelia in his arms.

There you have it. More words are spoken so that the unbearable becomes more unbearable, but that vision of Lear holding his dead daughter is not going away. The dead girl in the village shouldn't go away, but she shouldn't be everything because no one thing is everything. All the people on all these buses are telling me that and I'm trying to listen. And if it chokes me up, and will always choke me up, when I read the end of the play, if it takes me to this exhausted place where human beings have done too much and talked too much and seen too much, then that's okay. For me, *King Lear* is like one of those necklaces some guys wore to keep off the bad, death-dealing spirits. The play is full of bad spirits, terrible spirits. That comforts me. I'm not alone in this. The unbearable welcomes me.

For a white boy, you got some crazy shit in you, Tom, said Knightley.

I stare dully out the window. A lot of surveyors worked hard to make all these lines and towns and states. Everything is owned. But it isn't. One day we came into this other village and I got it— this is a village; these people live here together. I tried to explain it to the other guys but they looked at me like I was ridiculous. Someone, maybe it was Stone, said, who the hell wants to live together? And I understood him because in America no one has to live together. You can live apart. You're supposed to live apart.

We were fighting for the right to live apart, none of that communal nonsense for us, each one of us maxing out our personal pronoun, our golden mine.

Is that what you call a pun, Tom? Shit.

We didn't set fire to that village though. It escaped us. How about when in the early '60s we put people in hamlets, a nod to Shakespeare, right?

My mind is perturbed. Great thing of us forgot!

Forgot?

I saw the headline in the paper at the newsstand in Wheeling about the Wall Memorial being open for business. That's not the phrase they used, of course. They used something more official. Important people were going to bless it. Speeches. Healing. Memory. Forever. Bravery.

Do I sound hurt and angry? Tough shit. Very tough shit.

Am I going to visit? Maybe. I'm a living wreathe. Lear was decked out in the play like some kind of living wreathe. Cuckooflowers. There's a metaphor for you. I wonder where I can find some.

Look at that weird old man there. He's too old to have been in 'Nam. Maybe his son served. And what about that other old man with the heavy dark glasses? He's blind. He's moving his fingers along the names. Edgar. Edmund. There are a bunch of them, though, and anyway you have to go by surnames. The blind man is talking to someone named Tom who keeps saying his heart is breaking.

We get a rest stop in Hagerstown. It's another town that's decided it didn't want to be a town anymore, that it wanted to be a place for cars to live. I died for vehicular traffic: waiting at the light, running a yellow, accelerating, reluctantly braking. Car freedom.

I call the hotline and get the professor's wife.

Mike is in the hospital. He had a mild heart attack. I'm sure he'd like to talk with you later. No, no, he likes to talk with you. He's told me. You actually care about what he cares about. He's told me. It's like you live in the play, which is maybe a bit overdoing it but praiseworthy. You take it seriously and really you should meet some of his students. A few weeks ago, a girl—probably I'm supposed to call her a woman—raised her hand and said she found *Macbeth* to be boring. Imagine how Mike felt? And he's very polite. If it were me, I'd say how this play's been around for hundreds of years. What do you know from that? When they say "boring," they mean they can't be bothered to make an effort. No wonder Mike finally got sick. He takes medicine for his condition but stupidity gets on his nerves.

Thanks, I say, for filling me in.

Not a problem. I'll tell Mike you called. He'll be back. You can't keep a good Shakespeare scholar down. Bye, Tom.

I'm left holding the receiver and peering into not an abyss but certainly a deep well. It's not death's marauding presence that blanks me out but the ever-present bodily frailty. Flesh is thin stuff: easy in civilian life, everyone trundling along from day to day, to disremember.

Thou'dst shiver like an egg; but thou dost breathe.

There's that terrible glint of mockery: you think you know and you don't. The play is littered with it. There is no firm ground. Gloucester's suicide is a joke because the earth underneath him is a joke and falling is a joke and getting up is a joke. All the explanatory laws have run off and are nowhere to be found. Nothing to do but howl.

Hey, mister, I need to make a call. How 'bout it?

A short man in a rumpled suit, tie unloosened, is speaking to me.

The importunate moment gathers itself, explodes.

And here it comes. I start bawling. I run-stagger outside where, across a few hills and mountains, a Technicolor sunset is underway.

I stand there heaving and making squealing sounds, terror or some approximation thereof wringing my lost soul. It's not death that is doing this but survival. The professor walking into his class and recognizing another hand that tells him that he or she is bored.

Bored? The surest sign of mental failure. I look at the sunset with its orange and pink highlights, one more ultimate light show. All this is here for us each day and you're bored? Maybe I'm crying, too, for joy. I never think about that. People do it. I've read about it.

I compose myself, which means walking away a distance from the bus station and blowing my nose and wiping my eyes and looking again at the sunset that is still going on, a routinely unfathomable performance. I bow to the west. I stand there. I remember the bus is leaving soon. I wipe my eyes again. I hate to leave the sunset but it's leaving already anyway.

The guy who asked for the phone is still talking or, from the sound of his voice, arguing. It must be love or money that's got him that worked up. It's love. I hear him as I cross the station floor: Look, Sandra, would I lie to you?

Look, Sandra, would I tell the truth to you?

On the bus, I try to think of my first words to Paula. I mean beyond "hi." We're not spontaneous. We're more like dutiful. And I'm more like a project. I have this brother and he was in the war, he got drafted because he got kicked out of college for a really half-assed reason, but he went and then got screwed up the way a lot of them seem to have gotten screwed up and he sort of wanders around now and he does menial jobs, which he doesn't really seem to mind, but he can't focus. He's smart in a humanities-sort-of-way and he's been like this for a long while, I mean over a decade, and I talk to him and he seems to listen, but it's like he's on some orbit that doesn't include the rest of us here on earth and he's addicted to a play by Shakespeare which is—and he'll be the first to tell you—a tragedy. There it is—a tragedy. It's not a word you can do much with, which seems to suit him.

Hi, I say to Paula. She walks up to me. Paula strides more than she walks though. And even when she meets her vagabond brother in a bus station, a place she never would set foot in otherwise, she's dressed in casual clothes that tell you they are purposefully casual. They cost money to be casual.

Still got that jacket? She says by way of a greeting. She gives me a peck on the cheek. She's a serious lipstick woman among many, many other things. She's shorter than I am by quite a few inches but she's got her heels on. She's a woman of heights.

I'm attached to it, I guess.

It's not the only thing you're attached to.

Whoa! It happens that fast. I can get back on the bus, I say. I'm going to Baltimore next week to meet a documentary filmmaker. He's making a movie about Vietnam vets and he wants to talk with me. I can go to Baltimore. I hear myself: obstinate, frightened, sick with fraught hope. Hey, how about a hug?

You owe me no subscription.

She moves up to me and buries her head in my chest. Her grip around me is strong. Mine is, too.

When she pulls back, she takes a look. My little brother is getting older, she says. Is that gray in your lovely brown hair?

I've been meaning to get some Clairol or some shit like that. One guy I knew turned white overnight.

A scrutinizer, she's still looking at me. There's always "one guy" isn't there? And then there's you. You're one guy, too.

That's how it works, isn't it?

How what works? The laws of thermodynamics, the lives of men, the playing out of mass democracy in a jungle?

Why don't we get a bite? She says. You've probably been sub-sisting on candy bars and American cheese on white bread. There's a Chinese place near my apartment that I go to a lot. You're prob-ably okay with Asian food, right? And she smiles her sharp smile.

Paula is the sister closest in age to me in the sister line-up. She was four when I was born. She's always been at a distance but near. I was a kind of a toy to her and she tyrannized me, telling me how things were and what I was doing wrong. Still, I loved her and I suppose she loved me in some bossy, sisterly way. You get stuck in these things in families. You revert, to use a word I've heard from a VA counselor, but I'm not sure I'm reverting because I'm not sure I ever moved on to begin with.

I still want to know what Paula and I mean to one another. That's the question Cordelia is asking at the beginning of the play after her sisters have protested their empty love. Cordelia's "nothing" is asking—behind why are you doing this, Dad, making us make a show of love—what do I mean to you? I'll tell you what you mean to me but you must tell me what I mean to you. But what if the person being asked doesn't know? What if the person is a man who is too busy being a man to know what anything means to him? Cordelia doesn't understand that. She feels that love is like water that flows and fills in all the crevices, smoothes the hard edges. Men, though, are serious dam constructors, and some women, too, like her sisters.

Some of these guys, I expect them to beat on their chests like Tarzan. Me American! You Gook! said Knightley.

Tom, I'm over here.

I look around. It's a low-décor Chinese place, a few paper lanterns to evoke the mysterious Orient, a few scroll-like paintings of men and women in elaborate robes and remarkable hair-dos.

You staying long? She asks. I just need to know. I'm involved with someone and actually I'm spending a lot of time at his place, so you can stay as long as you like, but you know me. I like to know these things. Though knowing you; you may not know yourself, my tumbleweed brother.

So what do I mean to you, Paula, in the scheme of things? I plant my elbows on the table and cup my chin in my hands.

You didn't answer my question. She puts her hands on the table, palms down, and draws her back up.

A waiter comes who brings tea with him and takes our order. I pour some tea and take a sip. It's weak.

A tumbleweed doesn't know much about the future, I say. So I've answered that. What's your answer, sis? You know how little brothers are—full of questions.

When we were children, you were always there. And then I went off to school and into what became my life. She picks up the tea cup and cradles it in her hands like an offering but doesn't drink. And I became fuller of me.

You were always pretty full of yourself. I smile.

I left myself open to that one so I agree. She sets the cup down. When I would come home, it was as if I had to remember who you were. It wasn't anything about you. You were in high school doing what people do in high school. It was about me. I could feel you receding. It bothered me, but it's nothing I ever talked to you about because I was so excited to be living my life. You know, a life not bounded by living in the house I grew up in. And then you went off to college and I went to graduate school and was focused, very focused on what I wanted to do.

What is it you do, by the way? More smiling.

Look through a microscope. Ever use one?

I wanted to screw my biology lab partner real bad. That's all I can remember.

Sounds right. She picks up the cup and takes a sip. I guess I don't go here for the tea, she says. She makes a face of distaste that I remember right away from the dining room table when we were children. A little tremor goes through me.

And then you went off to that war, and even though I wrote you a letter now and then, I felt—what could I say? And even though you wrote something now and then—what could you say? It was a strange feeling because I usually have the words and you haven't been lacking either. But there just didn't seem any words, beyond *don't get killed*. That's not much of a letter. Or a conversation after-wards, like *Well, you didn't get killed, that's good.* I mean I was relieved that you came back because I had this black knot of dread inside me. But when you came back it was like someone coming back from the far side of the moon. It wasn't anything I could understand or maybe even anything that I wanted to understand. I was living my life and putting together my career and living with Steve.

He was a long-timer wasn't he? Nice guy.

He was a long-timer, that's right. Nice guy but . . . I won't go into that. And then you started drifting and I never heard much from you. It was episodic and your voice on the phone didn't sound like your voice to me. It was someone else's voice. Paula looks around. I'm hungry, too. Do you want to hear all this, Tom?

I'm listening. I've sat in a lot of circles at the VA where we divulge our contents. I can listen.

See what breeds about her heart.

So we're sitting here now and I don't have the dread in me but I have something else in me. Maybe it's despair. Maybe it's a feeling that I lost you even though you're sitting right across from me. And it's a feeling that it's more my fault than yours because you went to a place and I didn't follow you.

Follow me? You mean enlist?

I don't mean enlist, no. Her turn to smile. I mean you just felt so far away from me that I gave up. I figured there were too many miles there.

The waiter shows up. My appetite seems to have vanished but the pork-whatever-it's-called that I've ordered smells great.

I like to get things done, Paula says. I like things to be as clear as I can make them. I spend my days working to see if something goes a certain way and why it goes that way or why it doesn't. There are a lot of variables. But with you I haven't known what should be done. Not just because it's your life and none of my business, however much I'm your overbearing sister. It's bigger than that, way bigger. She looks down at her plate. She's got a shrimp-something. I guess you should talk. I'm ravenous.

I appreciate your words, sister. I feel all formal. I feel that my life is standing beside me and looking on. Tom went out on the heath and got lost. He came back but he still was lost. He says something at the end of the play, as if he knew what he was doing, but he doesn't. It's only because the audience expects him to speak: time to wrap things up, folks, and go home. Beat the traffic across the Thames.

I'm glad to be here with you now eating Chinese food. I guess that's what I have to say. I put down my chop sticks. I can feel my face puckering. There's nothing like losing it in a Chinese restaurant. Dish too spicy? Asian flashback?

Paula reaches a hand across the table and takes mine. We make a little bridge, careful not to let our hands plop into our food. Her face is puckered, too. We squeeze each other's hands and pull back. Then we both exhale like when we were children whirling around in a circle in the backyard and about to fall down. Sometimes we did fall down.

You're someone that something has happened to. It's put you in a different category. It's not that I'm uncomfortable with it—

No?

No, that's not it. It's the distance. It seems permanent.

So I'm a victim and you're not.

Victims don't pull triggers, do they? Paula grimaces but tries to change her face. How's your dish, Tom?

Comfortable, I say.

Oh, dear brother, I'm sure I say the wrong things but you have to allow me my frustration. And while we're in that place why don't you explain to me one more time your attachment to a certain play by William Shakespeare. Before you show up I always take a look.

> Be governed by your knowledge, and proceed
> I' the sway of your own will.

I try to do that, Tom. Paula looks down and gives a sisterly sigh.

No offense, I say, but knowledge is oversold. It's one reason I never went back to school. Robert McNamara—one bright guy, brains on top of brains. So what? He couldn't see past the end of his educated nose. I point to my plate. Great food, oh, savvy sister.

You sort of like treading near the abyss, don't you? There's the sustaining of life and then there's you in the play, who is someone who is a victim, wronged by his brother, impugned, lied to. So he flees.

Nice you keep reading the play. I can feel myself collapsing. It's been a long day, I say.

Paula frowns, pushes at the food that's left on her plate, and then leans toward me. I'm not a big wisher but I wish we could talk like when we were kids. I could talk for hours with you.

Mostly you were telling me what to do and how everything and everybody in the universe worked but, yeah, we did talk and I looked up to you. I still do.

Tom will throw his head at them.

I guess I expect something to issue from our words, Paula says. Something between the large talk of the play and the small talk of how was your day? Is that wrong?

It's not wrong, I say. You're used to results. I'm not. At the end of the play the people who are still alive are dazed and semi-destroyed.

She looks past me. Back to my apartment now? She asks and waves at the waiter to get the check. Your fold-out bed is unfolded. I'll be sleeping elsewhere.

I lean back. You've never let any grass grow under your feet.

We're not here to make lawns, Tom. You know that better than anybody. All that running around on the heath, whatever else it is, it's energy.

When Paula closes the door on the way out of her apartment, I'm lying in bed and feeling how much I need to pick myself up. I've felt it a few thousand times before and I've tried. It's not just about going to work each day. It's the believing part that's hard. It's like I read a page I wasn't supposed to read and I can't forget it, the girl-coming-toward-you page. But there's no *supposed* and I know that. I know, too, I'm not going to sleep. I've been waiting to call Doreen.

Hi, dodo, she says. You just blow into town? Got a girl on a string you're aiming to pull? Some poor female who hangs around the house and mopes, waiting for a vagrant to knock on her door and show her a miserable time?

I take it you may not want a visit from me tonight.

Of course I'd like to wander around the Mall with you, dodge spirits, and howl at the moon. What better time could a girl want? Cavort in the aftermath of the scariest play of all-time? I will say that although Edgar seems on the clueless side of the street, he does change into Tom; I have to give him credit for that. He has an imagination.

When Edgar is Tom, he's Tom. Edgar's gone.

That's a bit cryptic.

I'd just like to take a bite out of you, Doreen. Tonight.

You do know how to court a lady. I wish I were a poet.

Keep hanging with me.

You have to be around for me to do that.

Can you come by here, Doreen? My sister took her car.

Can I get out of bed and get into my car and drive to wherever you are and walk in and say, No trouble at all, long-lost lover boy? No, I can't. Goodnight, sleep tight. Call me tomorrow, when you can take a bus here. I'm off from work. Maybe I'll bake some brownies or come to the door naked. Or both.

Smile you my speeches, as I were a fool?

Doreen isn't naked and I don't smell brownies when she opens the door. She stands there in a man's tee shirt (not one of mine) and blue jeans and looks me over. A number of emotions seem to play across her face. The truth of them would be poetry, something about midsummer and something about autumn dusk, the time of year now when the year is preparing to die. And something about wind on the water, the water creasing and wrinkling.

Why are you so hard? She asks. I know the answer but some-times I have to ask the question for my own sanity so I can pretend there is no answer. I can pretend he's just a wandering boy because you know I don't give a crap about your holding a steady job or having a checking account because I know you've worked plenty. You painted this house a few summers ago, if you recall.

I do. Can I—

Not yet, no, you can't. This is my house and you are a lowly peti-tioner. A varlet. How's that for a word? What a brazen-faced varlet, thou art, except you aren't brazen-faced. Most people get thicker, their flesh getting tired, but you seem to be getting softer and thinner. Maybe some memories are letting go of you, or am I indulging in wishful thinking here at eleven o'clock in the morning on my one day off this week?

I can't say about the memories. Or I can. They're there. They have to be.

But they don't have to throttle you, dodo, do they? You've paid your share of dues.

I want to yell at her and kiss her so I'm cancelled out and stand there saying nothing but I have to say something. The Shakespeare professor that I talk to, the guy I visited in Illinois, had a heart attack. He's okay, though.

Sorry, but happy the professor is still here. And you?

Oh, working out on the treadmill in the men's room in assorted bus stations. Regular 5K in the middle of the night. Actually in Fort Wayne, not long ago—

Don't tell me your shit, Tom. Really, honey, I've heard enough true adventures from you for one lifetime.

And you, Doreen?

I know not what the matter is.

Job's okay. I like animals better than people so I'm safe on that account. And of course what some people do to animals makes me like people even less, though lots of people love their animals

121

plenty. My love life's been flagging. I think I wore out random sex a while ago. Or maybe I just wore out guys coming on to me, how I can predict the whole evening within thirty seconds, if that long. What a mistake it is to let men run the world. I know two of Lear's daughters are bad news but he started it, right? My two Corgis are great. I talk with my mom once a week and we usually don't get into an argument. My car doesn't sound good. The engine's got some unhappy knock when I accelerate. I've started to learn how to cook Indian food. I considered going on an anti-depressant last month but couldn't quite pull the chemical trigger. And I'm on the verge of crying but it's not about you. It's more about me standing here telling you all this. What else do you want to know?

Well—

Why don't you come in out of the cold? That stupid jacket can't be keeping you warm. It's a mess in here. Actually it's not bad, that's my mother talking through me. My mom would have made Dolley Madison hang around to apologize to the British for any dust in the White House.

You drink a lot of coffee this morning, Doreen? You seem a little rattled.

I'm surface-rattled as opposed to deep-rattled.

You referring to me? Doreen leads me into her living room. Her dogs, who were lolling on a couch, get down and start jumping at my legs and barking.

They recognize you. It's the long-lost Tom, explorer of bus terminals, connoisseur of brown bag lunches, and willing ear to the woebegone, the bored, and the Biblical.

Doreen—

Can't you see I'm talking because if I stop talking, whatever glue is holding me together at this moment will unglue?

I take a step toward her.

Touching me now isn't a great idea. You aren't trustworthy. She turns to the dogs, tells them to calm down, then turns back to me.

What are the names of the dogs in *King Lear*? I love it that there are dog names amid all that people craziness.

Trey, Blanch and Sweetheart, I say. Lear's hallucinating. It's another kind of heartbreak.

As if there wasn't enough heartbreak to go around already? Some extra has to be made up? I help to put down animals almost every day and I see people cry like you wouldn't believe. Or maybe you would. But I think beyond heartbreak, because there's always something beyond everything, there's numbness. And I have to tell you that's what I feel with you sometimes. And it scares me because it's a place I can't reach. No one can.

I guess I invite this, I say.

Look, Tom, I've got a very big topic on my mind. Doreen clasps her hands together like she's about to start singing at the end-of-the-year school assembly. What I've been thinking—and she raises her hands—is that I want to have a child. And I want to have that child with you. That doesn't mean I'm proposing anything more than that. I'm not creating a married-dad scenario here. But I don't want it to be random. And I don't want science in-between. Whatever you are, you're natural.

I'm speechless, I say.

I don't want to lay a speech on you—and Doreen unclasps her hands—life has handed you too many already. I definitely don't want you to give me a speech. You might look, however, somewhere beside the past—like the future.

If you don't mind, I'm going to sit down. I'm a little wobbly.

Feel free but why don't you just say "yes" and we'll leave it at that? You don't have to make a mountain out of some fornications. If—

I guess—and I pause because I'm not sure what I guess. I don't say anything. I start to cry, not from the freaked-out, permanent heebie-jeebies but some place elsewhere, light rushing toward me from the darkness.

Doreen comes over and puts a hand on my head. I don't want any tears around my baby, she says.

Sorry, I say. I take a few gasps.

And then there are the words. You probably know them.

> When we are born we cry that we are come
> To this great stage of fools.

I do, Doreen says. It's okay—the words and me knowing them, both things. I understand they're not using them to greet moms in the obstetrics ward; though—as you've pointed out to me—there are lots of good qualities about fools. Among the things I treasure about you, dodo, is that your misty eyes, in their funny way, are wide open.

Are they?

Open enough to see me. Doreen sits down. Look at me.

I'm sort of dry heaving. Her tee shirt says 'Plant a Tree Today.' Do you mean what your tee shirt says? I ask.

I do, she says.

All my history—

No more than anyone's. No more than the brother who's wronged by his brother who's been wronged by his father, who becomes blind because blindness is more than a metaphor.

> Our debilities depend.
> Our longings stray but return at day's end.

I could have said that.

Maybe you will. With that, she takes off the tee shirt and starts to pull off her pants. I mean business, Tom.

I do too, I say.

When I get back from here, I'm gonna have a whole mess of children. Ain't one of them going into the army either, said Knightley.

Our bodies become our voices.

And afterward we make no plans.

The neighborhood that Knightley's mom lives in isn't rundown but it's not run-up either. For me, who grew up on the north shore of Boston among Irish, Italians, and WASPs, it has that feeling of This Is Where the Negroes Live because it's true: it is where they live, thanks to more bleak history than any of us can hold in our hats. It haunts me because it's like a whole other story going on that is so accepted it's not a story, but some kind of condition or weather. There were wars. There were slaves. There were screams that went on for centuries. Even in daylight, walking along a street that has some trees on it and little lawns and front steps with pots of geraniums, it's haunting. The capacity of human beings to endure grief is impressive. Ask any tragedian.

If there be more, more woeful, hold it in.

I've got a piece of paper with a house number on it. Knightley and I have been sporadic correspondents. He's so with me every day that writing him has always seemed strange and beside the point, way beside the point. Of course, we're all supposed to help each other adjust or adapt or let it all out or whatever it is we've been doing since fighting what Knightley called, in one of the few letters he wrote me, The War That Went Nowhere.

For I am almost ready to dissolve.

I stop, read the house number, walk up the cement front steps and knock on the door, a couple of light raps. The door has two raised panels that run down the length of it. Some carpenter made this door.

The face that greets me doesn't exactly greet me.

What is your business? A woman asks me. She looks me over then makes a clicking sound. I know who you are, she says. You're Tom, aren't you? You're Tom, she says again, as if in something like amazement. You knew my boy. You were a friend to him.

He was a friend to me, Mrs.—

Alberta, you can call me by my name. She has a scarf wound around her hair that trails down her back. She's wearing a house dress but she has on jewelry—a big necklace with some turquoise in it and some silver bracelets. You come on in. She makes a welcoming gesture and pulls the door back some more.

I came to ask about your son. I'd like to see him.

Alberta tips her head a sudden bit and I feel it—not that she's thinking hard but because her head might fall off.

There's no way 'round it. My boy's dead.

I—

He got shot to death. He was standing on a street corner talking with some friend of his and some people drove by and started shooting. They were trying to kill the other man but they killed my son. The other man, he lived. Her head is still tipped. It's too much to stand up straight. Death comes and puts you at an angle.

Here it goes again. Tell the gods to stop.

I'm sorry. I'm really sorry. I'm going to cry, Alberta.

With a jerk, she pulls herself up, shuffles the few steps to me and hugs me. Then she's crying, too. There we are: two bodies in a hallway, clutching, wailing, and drowning.

> This would have seemed a period
> To such as love not sorrow; but another,
> To amplify too much, would make much more,
> And top extremity.

After a small eternity, she pulls back. You come in here and sit down, Tom. I thought I might be done with crying. I thought all I had was this heartache, this hole in me, but here I am tearing up. I got two girls and I love them but he was my boy. He came home from that war and did the best he could. Whatever it looked like to other people, he did the best he could.

She has an abstracted look in her eyes. She's talking to herself: monologue delivered to another person. I know the genre.

I can't tell you what it was like to watch that coffin go into the ground after all the worry I had when he was away. When he came home, I thanked the Lord a million times over.

Now she sees me.

But it's one *thank you* at a time, I guess.

I grope my sniffling way into what another century would have called "the parlor." It's neat and there are photos everywhere. Right away I recognize one of Knightley, probably around the time he enlisted. He's smiling for the camera. One of Knightley's amused expressions when some shit came down was "Little did I know."

Your son was more than a friend to me. He was a teacher. He was a little younger than I was and I teased him about that but—

I can feel myself getting lost. Regroup, Tom.

He kept his head straight. It was easy there to lose your head. I lost mine more than once. I try to make a good-natured smile, a perform-for-the-world smile, but fail. I'm still trying to find it, Alberta—my head, I mean. I make a sound—*whew*.

Looks like it's there to me. She makes a sad chuckle. We got to go with what we have. She waves vaguely at the room. I got my daughters and they have children and that's good because children are life. But I don't have my son. Once more, the words to herself.

Part of me wants to get up and run through the door and keep running. I hate that in myself. It's worse than fear. It's the wanting to stop my ears so I don't hear any more words ever again, all those confused announcements. I twitch but stay put.

I'm sorry to have been the one to tell you, Tom. You come here looking to see Jason out of the goodness of your heart and look at what you've got—another Negro killed by a Negro. You wouldn't know about that and it's just as well. She makes an unbearably sad face. Don't I wish I didn't know?

Look, Alberta, I say. Your son kept me alive. I don't mean he pulled me away from some bullet with my name on it like in the movies. I mean he talked to me. He took me under his wing and he sort of kept me there. Sometimes, now, I think I've had it with people talking about anything. It's just bullshit. Excuse me, I didn't mean to swear.

Alberta makes a dismissive motion, a little signature in the air. I've heard worse, she says.

But talking with your son kept me alive and instructed me about how to live, not just then but after.

So you—

I can't say I do anything special. I travel around, see America. But I'm here and that's because of your son.

You lucky then. You lucky. Alberta looks puzzled.

Oh, oh, oh! There's that horrible pain—me alive, her son dead, me talking to her, her son silent in the earth, a thought in her head. Oh!

> He fastened on my neck, and bellowed out
> As he'd burst heaven.

We're both quiet.

Don't cower, Tom. Don't hide in a happy hollow.

I need to get you something to drink, Tom. You come to my house—what kind of hostess am I? I could make you a cup of good coffee, the real stuff they grind for you at the grocery. Alberta gets up but doesn't move further. I'm telling you the truth. You come here today out of the blue sky and I need you to sit here and talk about my boy. You hear me? I need you to talk to me. You can do that, right? She thrusts her head forward, beseeching.

Gather yourself up, Tom. That's something yet.

I can do that a bunch, I say.

My son was no angel. If he wasn't out there talking to some no-account, he'd still be here. He had a lot of goodness in him, though. Not the church kind. I admit that. He had no use for the church and that pained me because he was brought up holy. All my children were brought up holy. But Jason was a different kind of person. When he was little, he was always asking me "Why this" and "Why that."

He was like an inventor, someone who could take life apart and then put it back together.

Yeah, that was my boy. A good head on his shoulders. But he had some of the fool in him. He could be foolish. He didn't know how to look after himself. I'd tell him, but a mother telling a grown man what to do—that don't play.

I rose above my shudders and told her stories about her son. She listened and sometimes she smiled but it was grievous work: time puddling at my feet, me looking for someone who was not there.

You heard about that wall? She asked when we were both standing by the door. They say it's something, right there in the middle of all the monuments, all the famous people. I guess everybody has to see it, can't miss it. You must know some names on it.

I do.

I lie in bed at night, she says, and wish I could take back what's happened. It only makes it worse but that's how I feel. He couldn't find one thing that made him happy. If he could have found that thing, maybe he wouldn't have been on that street corner. Maybe he would have been far away from here, sitting in some office, people listening to what he had to say. He had so much to say, always talking.

Her eyes implore but I can do nothing.

Thank you for coming by. Thank you for thinking of my son. I know he wasn't much of a letter writer.

Neither was I.

He talked about you sometimes, though. I have to tell you, he laughed sometimes about you. You know what Tom did one day? He'd say.

Couldst thou save nothing?

I took a couple of buses to get to Knightley's house but I start walking. I can't sit next to anyone. Wherever my legs take me, they take me. Various voices bang around in my head. There's a newscaster, someone on television who projects the image that This Person Is Serious, who intones that Jason Knightley survived Vietnam but not the streets of our nation's capital, and goes on to tell a sad tale from which we are supposed to learn what? That Jason should have stayed in the army because it was safer. That Jason should have moved away from Washington to one of the top ten places for white people to retire and worked as some sort of lackey but been safe. That Jason should have stayed in a bedroom in his mother's house and become a Negro Boo Radley. That we have to fill up the news with Stories of Head-Shaking Irony that allow you to have something to say to your partner later in the evening beyond we haven't had sex in four months.

Then there's Alberta's voice, that spirit-depth like "Go Down, Moses," a hymn Knightley used to hum, but with an edge that gives me chills. She knew her son was lost. It was only a matter of time. Even a natural death was only a matter of time, too much bearing down on him. He was never going to be sitting in that office somewhere, being safe, depositing his paycheck every two weeks and going home to the wife and kids where he watched TV and ate steaks. It wasn't that he had anything against TV or steaks. He would have been happy enough to get with that level of the game, but that level took a certain amount of belief, of having an unrattled cage, of living in the tunnel of your unimpeded happiness.

Knightley's is the voice I have most in my head—big man, big voice. I'd told him about the play plenty and we talked about it plenty, how things kept falling away until there was nothing left, how one trouble led to another. The play says that if you think you're going somewhere safe, you're wrong. You're born into the trouble that people make and then you die in that trouble. You can turn your head. You can pretend. You can try to become a master of the trouble. You can say you don't care. None of what you say matters. We knew that and a lot of people from that time, people like my sisters who had no use for the war, knew that. When I got back I protested against the war, too, but my words seemed small; even when all those people came together to march, the words felt small beside the trouble. When nations make the trouble it gets a lot bigger.

You marching, Tom? Knightley said. Well good for you. I hope the president takes you aside to have a little chat.

It didn't surprise Knightley that almost everyone was dead at the end of the play or that Cordelia died, too. Why shouldn't she die? He said. Everyone else was doing it. Imagine if you were here in this war and you thought your goodness was gonna protect you. Imagine how crazy that would be. Your man Shakespeare knew that.

Bless thy five wits, Tom's a-cold and getting colder.

I stop outside a little grocery store and then go in. The proprietors are Korean. They look me over. In this neighborhood that's what you do. I'm hungry but this isn't the place to do much about that, so I buy a PayDay, my go-to nourishment. They regard me skeptically—a particularly wan specimen of so-called humanity. Did my war help them get here? Or was it another war? How many lost varieties of the human race do they see each day? I say thanks again and stroll out into the remarkable sweetness of the light.

Being alive, nothing beats it, man. But I need to stop quoting Knightley. I used him, the way the innocent use the experienced, the way my skin took for granted what his skin never took for granted. I don't know what kind of shit he was into, maybe none, maybe some, but the kind of shit wasn't the point. The unlucky get unluckier. Every wise man has holes in him.

I stop at a phone and put in some coins. The professor picks up.

How are you? I say. My voice is on the delirious side. Take a breath.

Tom, yes, it's good of you to ask. The doctors say I'm good as new but I don't feel good as new. That's only something the doctors say. All that education they have. They're prideful people. Some of them could have been kings in Shakespeare, slinging assurances and commands, take-charge guys. But they don't have the true words, do they? But how are you? And where are you?

I'm at a phone in Washington. I'm a little shaky. I found out that a friend of mine from the war is dead.

Ah, Tom, I'm sorry to hear that. There's a mortal catch in Mike's voice. Is it that friend you quoted to me sometimes, the pithy one? What was his name?

Knightley. Yeah, that one.

From what you told me, he sounded something like a professor himself. But one who knew more about life. You wouldn't believe how imbecilic a lot of my job is. Whatever you're doing with your life, you don't have to sit through long, boring meetings that only lead to more meetings.

I can feel a sort of torrent mounting in me. How did Shakespeare understand everything to put it into words? I ask. How did he understand? I know it's a stupid question, professor, but I have to ask. It's sort of unbearable to me, how I carry this play around and it means so much to me but I don't know anything about who wrote it. It's never bothered me before—I mean who cares, the play is what matters—but right now, standing here, it bothers me because he was a person, not some god. He was a person.

I'm sorry, professor, if I'm babbling. I'm sorry.

There's silence on his end: the courtesy of thought, of taking me seriously. I could kiss his saggy, dark-eyed face right through the line.

He didn't know, Tom. He was curious about why people did the things they did. He treasured drama, life as a drama, and he never felt he had to go beyond that, never had to find an answer or faith. He sensed how one thing always becomes another, how nothing stays still, how opposition is a fact of our being here. He was, since you're asking me to speculate, a good-natured person. What do they say these days? He didn't take life personally. He took it intensely—to feel all those people he had to—but he understood he was only a player and then a writer. He was on the sidelines, making things up. He lived in the words but not through them. But I don't want to get carried away. It's easy to do that, what they used to call bard-worship. You noticed there's not a bust of him gathering dust in my office.

Tom, are you there?

I'm here, I say. I'm here, I repeat.

"Thy life's a miracle." He wrote that—a very dark joke, a Vietnam joke—quite a fall you took there, Gloucester—but a reminder. I take a bite of the PayDay. For whatever it's worth, I'm a bit calmer.

You think about it, Tom. We'll talk another day. You know when I sign off, I always want to give regards to someone but I don't know anyone in your life, even though you seem to be always traveling to visit someone. You must have a lot of friends and family.

You could send your regards to Doreen. That would be nice.

My regards then to Doreen. Bye.

I walk further, then stop in the middle of a block and stand there. The bard walked around like me. He wrote that life's a miracle.

Speak yet again.

I try to feel it. What else matters? Again is a miracle, too.

An old Negro gentleman—that would be the word—comes up to me while I stand there rooting and expanding myself. He has on a suit jacket, a blue tie held in place by a tie tack and on his feet he has a pair of what I think was once known as "spats."

You lost? He asks.

Yes and no, I say.

You lost then. Where you want to be?

Nowhere special. Right here's good, talking to you.

I see. You make that jacket?

I did.

You come from slaves, you think twice about freedom. The word gets thrown around. So I wonder what you mean by that—Freedom Is Hell. His voice is patient, schoolmasterly.

I'm asking for this. I know that. I don't blend.

Hog in sloth, fox in stealth, wolf in greediness, dog in madness, lion in prey.

War turns you inside out, I say.

I know something about that, he says. I was in the first one, the one they called The Great War. The army back then was segregated. You got to die an equal death though. He turns his head and makes a spitting sound but nothing comes out.

And what you are fighting for, I say, is only a word. No Viet Cong was on my front step pointing a rifle at me.

I'm following you, he says. He's back looking at me. He's old but he doesn't wear glasses.

Freedom is a word but hell is something you go through and you may keep going through because it's not a word. It's something that happens to you. You don't ask questions about hell. Freedom—there are lots of questions, almost nothing but questions. It's an elixir you can't swallow. And if you aren't free inside, what's the point anyway? Am I making sense to you, mister?

Some. My question was impertinent but your jacket invites queries. It does, doesn't it?

Beware my follower! Peace, Smulkin, peace, thou fiend!

Not everything makes sense. I've noticed that especially—and I mean no offense by saying this—with white folks. They frequently make unreal assumptions then are surprised. They want to be thanked when they've been of no help. Your name, sir, is?

Tom.

Good to have encountered you today, Tom. Too much talk rots the brain. I'll be seeing you. He begins walking away from me, leisurely but deliberate.

Maybe I need a new jacket, one that says: What Was That?

What are you there? Your names?

And which street was Knightley killed on? It was a heath, Tom. The sky was raging. The sky was still. Desolation was everywhere. Desolation spoke slowly so we could hear each word. It was this street and that one a block over. I have the directions to find it. There are no directions. You already are there. You will never be there. You weren't living his life. Were you living your own? Answer me that.

I pick up my duffel at Paula's. She's a note leaver. This one says: Do What You Need to Do. We'll talk. Later. P.S. The documentary filmmaker wants to see you here in DC.

I knock but barge into Doreen's.

Knightley's dead.

She's coming toward me from the kitchen. That's so bad. You and death—

Me and death, everybody and death—I can't begin to say how I feel but I need to try. I put my hands up to my head like I just was captured.

Please, Doreen, please.

Okay. She makes a motion as if cleaning her hands. Do you want a hug? Or no, let's sit down. Forget the hug. Talk. Dinner can wait.

Rumble thy bellyful. Spit, fire, spout rain.

His mom told me. He was shot. She said that the shooter was look- ing to hit the guy Knightley was hanging out with. It was on a street corner. Friendly fire. You know, Doreen, what the dumbest words are? The words *this isn't fair.* Those are the dumbest words because there is no book recording every right and wrong, every up and down. There isn't and everyone over the age of five knows that. Knightley was my compass, maybe a screwed-up compass standing on a street corner waiting to cop who knows what, but he was my man and for him to go through what he went through and then die like that—because he knew what it was like to be here one second and not be here the next—it way more than sucks.

The sound inside me feels much larger than a howl, as if only the earth's breath could make that sound. I'm a person and that's where I'm stuck—tinny, inconsequent, wordy. Don't be going boo- hoo about this shit, Knightley would say. But I'm boo-hoo.

Doreen lets me be. She's not out to maneuver my feelings. Maybe that's love, or at least, kindness.

Let it bleed, sirrah. There's the truth—let it bleed.

I quiet down but I don't feel better. Doreen, I say, I'm trying to take you in now. Right now. You're here. I know it sounds stupid but I'm trying. Do you understand?

Well—

You don't have to do anything, just your being here is good. I failed Knightley.

Tom—

No, I failed him. I could have been something more than a rolling stone. I could have stood up for him and done more than look up to him. I see his body on that street corner with the plastic laid over him. I see that. I know what that is. Oh, damn!

Doreen lowers her head. She sees it, too.

Or maybe that's some bullshit I'm telling myself because there were chasms between us, not just him being black and me white—that was the least of it in ways—though death was paying him back for being black, no doubt about it, but him being aware and me struggling, always struggling. I can't tell you how tired I am of struggling.

She picks her head up. She's got some tears. Actually you can, she says.

Okay then. You know how I think. In the play, Edgar doesn't know what hit him. His brother schemes and plots and Edgar gets played. That's the word Knightley used when I was doing one of my plot summaries with him—played. There's a lot out there that can play you—communism, democracy, capitalism, you name it, and Tom—in the play—same word, how's that?—he takes that on. He strips it down so he can feel how much can play you. And it does. He's out there quaking, shivering, and babbling. He's jelly. He has to somehow build himself up, redesign himself, but he doesn't know what he's doing. When people say he's cruel to his father, how he doesn't reveal himself to his father earlier, that presumes he knows what he's doing. People don't get how stripped down he is, how he's trying to reassemble himself but he doesn't know what his pieces are. He didn't know what he was doing in the past, just nodding along with his role. And he starts to learn new things that no one back in the unplayed world ever told him. What's he supposed to do with that? One day you're in a college dorm room trying to get friendly with some girl and the next day death is staring you in the eyes thousands of miles away. What the fuck happened? That's got to be one of Tom's ineloquent, unasked questions: What the fuck happened?

How bitter and cynic our tongues become.

What did happen, Tom? Doreen's voice is tentative. Her two dogs are lying on the floor near us. They're quiet in that way dogs get quiet when they're around human grief. It hurts them too.

Everything's in progress, but that's a poor word to describe what Edgar goes through. He turns into Tom and Tom will never leave him, no matter what he says at the end of the play. There's stuff that never leaves you, like the girl in the village.

True to tell thee, the grief hath crazed my wits.

I hear crazy sounds all around me. One of them is Lear's voice, almost more a bark than a voice. It can't be, of course, but it is. The king no longer a king—there it is.

The voices and sounds—

They are so real they aren't real. They're at the very end of the spectrum, like a color you can't see, that says it's a color but it's out there beyond black. Tom could probably make a rhyme about it.

He probably could. That's one of his gifts, isn't it? Alack and black. To hell and black, I say.

Now look at me, Tom. Doreen leans her face up to mine. Remember what you said? Well, I'm here. This—you, Knightley, the war that never ends—affects me, too. Do you understand? It's not just your shakiness that's here. It's mine, too, because I have my own share of it. And if you're thinking that here she comes: an understanding, sympathetic woman to the rescue, Mother Clara Barton, that wouldn't be me. It shouldn't be me. I can't make it go away. You know that. I'm not denying you. I'm saying that what made this sea of sadness is bigger than you and me. I'm not about to start bailing. I'm not—thank goodness— Cordelia either.

I would allow myself the luxury of grief.

> I would be quiet—a stone in a field, a tree,
> A spoon, a rug, all things told with stillness.

Our bodies—and Doreen leans in a little closer—are telling us to go forward. I'm sure Knightley would have agreed with me. I met him once or twice if you remember.

I don't. No, I do. There's a picture.

He was handsome in that way big guys can be handsome, sort of overwhelming but boyish. He was funny, too. He made me laugh. I remember that. I can almost remember some of what he said. He said something about you wearing a wristwatch.

We both look at my timeless wrist.

I own one, I say. It may be broken, though. I could get it fixed. I could buy another. Drugstores have big displays of watches. Timex, Bulova, I know my brands.

Doreen moves her hair back from where it's fallen onto her face. She has brown hair. You remember the slogan, Tom, make love not war?

More than one guy had it on his helmet.

Well, it's a sentiment that I agree with. Another hair flip, this one more seductive. Also a provocative hip jut. I'm in favor of feeling good.

Don't pull your tee shirt off yet, Doreen. And don't get me wrong—it's my kind of patriotism—but there's a lot in the way.

> Horns whelked and waved like the enridgèd sea.
> It was some fiend.

So for me to feel good—

And you distrust feeling good because it means you're letting down your guard, abandoning your act that is so deep it doesn't feel like an act. You were there before the war. You are here after the war.

Tom is in-between. He lies betwixt the bed's top and bottom. There the unlucky chambermaid can find him.

I want to make a baby. It's not words. I want to make a baby. Don't make me plead. Be a gentleman. There's no shortage of history on my side of this story either.

Tom is abandoned. He should be. What help is he? One more crooked finger pointing at whatever hurt him, trashed him, tried to ruin him. What help?

Forget the tee shirt. Take off your pants, I say.

Fie, foh, and fum.
Here I come.

The dogs watch for awhile but then lose interest.

Afterward, we don't put on our clothes.

I think that did it, Doreen says.

Plenty more where that came from.

It's nice to hear you brag. You tend to skitter and scatter.

Being naked, do you ever think about Adam and Eve?

All the time. I think about where we came from, if that's what you mean. Apes, worms, amoebas, Adam, Eve—I think about all of it. Dogs and cats, too, because I spend so much time with them.

And the primal soup?

What about it?

Is that what I just pumped into you?

I would hope so. I can feel the meeting going on down there.

Sixth sense?

The first one, I'd say. Doreen pats her private area.

I yawn and stretch. My underarms are good and ripe. I don't know if I want to talk to this documentary guy. He's from Holland.

You have something against Dutch people?

No. I like windmills and tulips and silver skates. I don't think I want to be documented though. It seems impossible. What I was is gone. What I'm now, someone talking about the past, seems pointless. Whatever I say is lackadaisical compared to what happened.

What am I going to do? Sit there and howl? This was my fear, Mr. Dutchman. I can act it out now but it's only a fraction, though it still can get me down on the floor, believe me. And I don't like the idea of it just being me. There should be ten voices talking at once, twenty, thirty.

No one could understand then.

That's my point. And it's wrong to talk to the living. It's the dead who should be speaking. They've got the truest stories. Everyone who's alive has to lie.

So out went the candle, and we were left darkling.

You planning a Lazarus act? Now you don't see me, now you do.

It's not right, I say. I don't blame the guy. It's natural to want to commemorate and investigate and words like that. I understand that but he couldn't understand. What happened was way more than someone showing up later with a camera and a sympathetic attitude.

You haven't even met him, Tom. Maybe you're getting ahead of yourself. You tend to do that.

Do I?

It seems to come from having a livable catastrophe in your bones.

What I'm trying to get at is that we expect certain people to lie and prevaricate, like politicians. And they do. But what I'm trying to get at is that the living always have to make a story to explain what happened. A thousand things could happen and it's only chance that this one or that one happens to you. It's what doesn't happen that's really the story, but it's not a story. It's just this swirling around of possibility, like cosmic gas, unhatched universes, alternative fates, all the darkness we shovel into the blithe word *luck*. Who keeps a diary of what didn't happen? How can I tell him that?

You just told me. Probably you can tell him. Look, I'm going to get dressed. I'm getting cold. And don't say it—Doreen's a-cold.

Come back soon, I say.

You're the one who's sketchy, dodo, not me. I'm possessed of average female desires. No cosmic gas here. She stands up and

140

presses her clothes to her stomach. You don't know how good I feel at this moment. I wish you could. She sashays off.

Lear is all into ownership. That's where the play begins, with ownership and transferring ownership. Kingdoms, dowers, territories, cares of state—but there is no ownership. That's what Lear has to learn. He doesn't want to learn it, but who does? Does he learn it? Does he learn anything? He gets shattered but that doesn't mean he learns anything. I knew guys who got shattered but they didn't learn anything. They were looking for a door that would let them out but there was no door so they kept trying to make up a door, like Lear at the end of the play believing that Cordelia is breathing.

Look there, look there—

I could use the professor to talk with but I don't move.

Tom isn't shattered. He's something else. He's free because he's making it all up but he's still caught because he's with other people—it's not a one-man show—who tell him he should do things like lead his dad to Dover. Tom can't really do anything. He can just act out, that's it. And he keeps acting out so when he's with his dad, who wants to kill himself, Tom can only keep acting. He can't stop and say, "Hey, dad, I'm your son and though you acted shitty to me I love you and we can be okay together." That would be another realm of being, not the one Tom's in.

I look down at my nakedness.

There's someone named Edgar, though, who becomes Tom, the way there was someone named Tom who became someone else in the war. I don't think Tom ever leaves Edgar. We don't get to see that because everyone is too devastated at the end of the play. It's too awful already. But maybe it's good that Tom won't leave Edgar. Maybe Tom knew something Edgar never could have known. What did I know? It's not that I got enlightened. I can hear Knightley laughing right now: Tom, he One Wise Dude. No, it's more like reality, a demented reality, intruded on me the way Edgar's liar brother

Edmund intruded on him and then other things—like his father being blinded—intruded on him.

That's the most demented moment in the play, when Gloucester's eyes are torn out. In war, though, that happens every day—cruelty for the sake of cruelty, tossing guys out of helicopters, cutting ears off, putting a gun to a guy's head and pulling the trigger, stuff you don't tell the folks back home about; though when that photo came out of the guy pulling the trigger on some captured guy's head the folks back home saw something real. They could push it away and they did, but they saw it, even if it was a photograph and they didn't hear the sound the gun made or see the shot man fall down or see the executioner look down at the corpse and walk away. They thought, I'm glad that's not me and I'm glad that's not my boy pulling that trigger. Or maybe they wished they could pull that trigger, killing someone like that, letting everything go. No more sun for you, mister.

Are you going to take a shower, Tom? Doreen asks.

I smell like you, what more could I want?

Flattery will get you everywhere. Should I ask you what you've been thinking or is that unwise?

The usual, but more than usual, maybe some light at the end of the hopeless tunnel. I ask you: How many died for that metaphor?

Your suffering unbecomes you. Let your face fall.

The Dutchman will ask me about my politics because they have politics in Europe while we have popularity contests. And, after all, we are a varied people pursuing our varied happiness. Communists are out to mess with our happiness. They wear gray and read Karl Marx at night and don't fuck.

Keep thy foot out of brothels, thy hand out of plackets.

That's not true, Doreen says as she comes into the room. They have colors, listen to rock 'n' roll and fuck. She's toweling her hair, one of those melts-me-down female motions, that hair being tussled.

It was so hard being without women. The fucking part, I mean.

142

Maybe you should speak, Tom, for the fucking party. That's a real party. Doreen makes a curtsey then drops the towel she has over her herself.

You are quite the floor show, I say.

I want a dancing child, she says. If it's a girl, I want a potential Rockette. Did I ever tell you the time my parents took me to Radio City Music Hall? The very name made me swoon. I was so unimportant with my plain brown hair and lack of breasts back in junior high school and then I was sitting there looking at the Rockettes kick their legs. The world can do what it wants but there's nothing like those legs. She raises a leg then picks up the towel.

Don't stop now, I say.

You were thinking something serious. I know you. The war was another kind of college. No wonder you haven't wanted to go back to school. The world has no degree to give you. It's got leg kicks though.

I was thinking about the documentary guy. I don't think I want to talk to him. I'll betray someone. I'll try to agree or I won't agree and I'll try to show how individual I am, which makes me puke.

> In nothing am I changed
> But in my garments.

Don't you think you're a bit hard on yourself? He wants someone to talk and he'll put you together with other people who talk to him or he'll dispense with you, and you'll be in oblivion where you're most comfortable anyway. You don't have to worry about your cover getting blown. Trust me.

Ease up, girl. I may not become a husband but I'm studying to be a father.

My female advice: don't brag about how you divided your kingdom. Talk baseball. Shoot an air rifle at nothing. Cry sometimes.

I'm set then. I can do all that.

Good. Children need fathers, though I have to say, dodo, I'm amused you used the *h* word. More than one girl has fallen off a cliff for that word.

Cliff, I say.

Cliff, Doreen says. That's one of my favorite parts of the play. They should perform that part on a prairie—flat as far as the eye can see. No cliff in sight, just the inner ones.

I'll talk to him, Doreen.

Good.

First, though, I talk with Paula. This time she has the pork-something and I have the shrimp-something.

You're staying with Doreen? That's her name, I believe. Paula's drinking a martini—forget the tea.

For the time being, I say. I like the tea. The faint taste is comforting.

I know you're fond of "the time being," Tom.

There are worse places. How about you? I ask.

Scientists work on projects and projects take time. Life has a way of getting mapped out when you do what I do. In one way it's steady. In another it's not because you're trying to find out something and you don't know exactly when that will happen. That must sound boring to you, the Knight of the Endless Bus Rides.

I do meet a certain slice of the human race: the interminably mild and the semi-desperate. No one who matters—my kind of people.

We dawdle along for the duration of our meal, not at ease but not at unease. We talk about our sisters, how Amy is bustling through life, how Evie has stopped looking for love.

You've been kind to me, Paula, I say.

Have I? She makes a pained smile. I have the feeling that I can never do enough for you, Tom. Not because you're asking because you don't ask for much of anything. It's because—I'll be blunt—you lost part of yourself and I think I should be able to find something to replace it. The way a scientist would think, I guess. Or a sister who loves you.

144

What if I didn't so much lose something as find something that I haven't been able to quite make part of my repertoire? You know—some lines I can't quite recite.

Fathom and half, fathom and half! Poor Tom!

Repertoire? She asks.

I mean part of how I can live.

Still not following you.

It's like a weight that you realize isn't a weight. Or it's a premonition, maybe, a very long premonition that has to do with your waiting to die, expecting to die, knowing you can die, and then you don't and you realize the premonition was something simpler like fear and fear has only one thing to say. It's persuasive but monotonous. And blind.

Watch out, Tom! Fear says that over and over but I have watched out. Tom gets an A in the watching-out department. So let's just say my repertoire could expand, though that doesn't mean I'm going to business school tomorrow.

I wouldn't expect you to, dear brother. Paula takes a sip then smacks her lips demurely.

Let's just say I'm retiring my jacket and going incognito.

Ah. And the fabled play?

The play, dear sister, is bigger than any repertoire. It holds me. I don't hold it. And it has more than enough room. Just this afternoon, I talked with the professor I've told you about and that came up, how he's been reading the play for much longer than I have and how he doesn't get tired of it, or think he's got it. It surprises the professor, how no one in the play is simply one thing. Their shadows have shadows.

Paula motions to a waiter. Couldn't things be a bit lighter? Couldn't a comedy suffice? Love baffled for a few acts and then victorious. Everyone making up and then going off to make a rumpus in bed.

He wrote those too. There were no land mines there though.

Paula picks up her pocketbook. It has a soft, expensive gleam—a supple leather sun. You're a corner, Tom, that I keep peeking around expecting to find I don't know what.

And?

I guess that's what I find—I don't know what. For someone in my line of work, that's humbling.

Outside, somewhere, the night begins to rave and shake. Dogs, people, trees all howl. Another war somewhere on earth. Who hears them, Tom?

I'm likely to become a father, I say.

That's what I mean, she says, about around-the-corner. Congratulations.

Motherhood entice you? I ask.

Not yet. I've still got some eggs in the basket. She signs the charge slip. Does this possibility change your attitude about anything?

Am I thinking mortgages and little league? No. Am I thinking of Doreen's stomach growing with part of me in it? Yes.

Which makes you feel what?

I'm glad for her. It's her call. Helping to bring another body—and that's only the half of it—into this—

Great stage of fools is the phrase, I believe.

Is something I have mixed feelings about.

That they're mixed seems a step up, brother. And the stage is "great." Don't forget that.

I think he's referring to size not excellence. More doesn't mean better.

The words contain everything, don't they, all the shades?

Yeah, but—

No, you've infected me, brother. Each word trembles with thought. I—

Next time, you pick up the tab. You can pay in the mundane ways, too. And I can be a poet.

Outside, the early evening sky over Connecticut Avenue is rinsed in a pale afterglow. We stand and admire the delicacy of its vastness.

Look up a-height. Do but look up.

The Dutch filmmaker isn't exactly a filmmaker. He works for television.

I'm making a documentary about the memorial. This comes after our names (he's Jan), small talk about coffee and coffee shops in America, how he came up with my name (your government has all your names and addresses) and whether it's always this brisk in November in Washington.

Have you been there yet? He asks.

No.

Are you going?

Yes.

I see, he says.

No offense, I say, but you probably don't. Or you couldn't. It's not your fault. It's like you're making a documentary, which I understand is well-intentioned, but I have to say it's a bad idea because it's going to allow people to sit and watch and listen to guys tell their stories and some experts talk about what happened and what's going on now and how this will help us heal and that has nothing to do with what happened; that is a violation of the ugly moments that were the war and not just the war but the people making the war, the politicians and the people who helped them. It's the ugly moments that matter and they're gone and unless you can find a way to retrieve them—and really why would you want to?—there's no point in making something that people can sit there and listen to and grunt at and turn the channel or get up to fetch a beer and then ask, so what happened while I was gone, anybody die or chat about at work the next day after the sports news and office gossip—see that 'Nam thing last night? That's wrong.

> Whiles I may scape
> I will preserve myself.

You have strong opinions, he says.

I should have opinions. I'd be a bigger loser than I even am if I didn't have opinions.

Jan sighs. That word—loser. It means someone who has lost something?

It's someone who has wandered away and keeps wandering. So he's lost in that way—mapless. And he's lost the story people tell themselves each morning, the my-life-makes-sense story, though other people—it's natural—assume he's one of them. But he isn't. He's impersonating a person. He got hollowed out.

I see, he says. He has a serious, angular face; the crevices of middle age have begun. I like him for that face.

So whatever I say is beside the point. I'll say something because you'll have questions but I feel I'm dishonoring myself and others. Acting normal is no good—oh, the war, yeah, no big thing. And acting abnormal creates the impression that's already in too many minds—'Nam guy, strange and touchy. Hears a dog bark and loses it.

Are you, who have been tossed about, are you strange and touchy?

Everyone has things in their head they don't forget. It could be something that happened to you on the playground when you were ten, someone pushing you down or you pushing someone down. It could be worse, much worse, but it doesn't matter in one way because it's there in your head and you've got it for all of your time on earth. So in that sense I'm not strange and touchy. But I'm not in the comparison business. I pushed and got pushed.

That's fair, he says. What I am trying to do is to allow people to say things like what you just said. How should I say it? I have no love of the predictable mouth. And I have a few things in my own head.

I push my chair back a bit. Doreen has told me before—you don't allow for anything to surprise you, Tom. And you're wrong.

There's no memorial for those things, though, he says. And it's different when the suffering belongs to many people. It's not just yours.

No, it isn't just mine.

We drink our coffee which is getting cold. He makes a slight face.

Sorry, he says, but much better in Amsterdam.

Look, I say, I like you, Jan. No one made you come here and do this, I know that. I don't want to seem like some impossible asshole to you. I push my cup away. What can I say? I've studied hard but I don't know anything. The war was a lot of people who kept saying they knew what they were doing but about what and for what? What I can't stand is every talking face on every screen. The show of our intelligence—it angers me. It offends me. How dare you? But it's no big thing. It comes easy: talking, shitting, eating, knowing.

Jan pushes his cup away.

So when in *King Lear*—it's a play I like, you've probably read it, because Shakespeare's a big deal all over the world—the fool gives Lear a hard time, what he's pushing against is that show, the whole crappy swamp-fuck of the Certainty-of-the-Moment that we—like the king—toddle around in each day but pretend doesn't stick to us.

And you, how are you doing in this what you call swamp-fuck? He asks. He smiles thinly.

Worse than most, I used to think. Now, I'm not so sure. The opposite of being stupid isn't being smart.

They'll have me whipped for speaking true; thou'lt have me whipped for lying; and sometimes I am whipped for holding my peace.

Perhaps, Tom, we could talk more. He hands me his stateside business card. I will be here for a month or so. You know, I hated the war when it happened. I still hate that war—how the United States inserted its mighty self, how it assumed a virtue it did not have—but I knew I needed to come here and talk to people and hear what they thought, now, after time has gone by. I needed to test my hate. Maybe that makes sense to you? He raises his eyebrows. His face twists in puzzlement.

My anger and your hate—sounds like we could be friends, I say. We shake hands and on the street I point him in the direction of his hotel.

I stand there amid the busy people coming and going on their errands, their mouths open, their mouths closed, and a half-block away I see Knightley walking toward me. He's walking with the girl I shot. She's actually a little behind him but she's there. They pause together, a moment I can feel, like the wind on my face. They look at me; at ease, as the army would put it. The girl has to look around Knightley. He's so big.

You tired, Tom? Knightley would say. Well, you gonna get more tired. You gonna get so tired that waking gonna be like sleeping.

It's happened before, a moment that doesn't fit with the others. Or all the moments don't fit with this one huge, exceptional sliver. "The poetry of incomprehension," the professor called it when I told him about it. "Shakespeare excelled at it."

You don't say of an apparition of two dead people on a street in downtown Washington "then they were gone" when they never were there. I get that. Their space is infinite; ours isn't. Though they are voiceless, they are speaking our parts for us, my part for me. "Thanks," I say aloud but softly. "Thanks."

Do you believe in spirits?

> The sky speaks ungently, the birds would flee
> Their element. Death quickens the air.
> Fathoms open.

Breathless but trying to hold it together, I spill my events out to Doreen over some Thai food I've managed to remember to bring to what I've started to call "home," since I've moved my duffel bag in with her. When I tell her that I saw Knightley with the girl, she puts down her forkful of green curry.

You saw them?

Why wouldn't I see them?

You've got a point there, dodo, she says. You're more than a candidate, though being awake and dreaming could get you arrested.

Probably *dreaming* isn't the right word but you're a vet, so they're a little more likely to go easy on your undefined mental space. I can hear it: Well, Tom, you're wacked out but you did your bit for the free world. Just don't make trouble. Stick your head in this stock and keep it there for a couple of decades and we'll shuffle you off to an old age home, where you can tell lies to young girls. Old Tom, he's a hoot. He fought in some war back, you know, a long time ago. He sees things. Ghosts 'R' Us.

Time swallows our perils, fades our joys to baubles.

You're making fun of me.

Only partially, the antic part, your un-straightjacket. The other part is more post-everything sadness that I can accommodate in my modest abode. For you to see them both together, Knightley and the girl, on what, Pennsylvania Avenue in broad daylight, even by your freaky standards—

I—

Don't go into it. I don't know if you're telling me about a blessing or a nightmare and I don't care. I've parsed enough un-random craziness. I can feel life inside me. Whoever comes out I want to start with a good outlook, no dark vibes, please, no visions from the ether. There'll be time for innocence to be lost.

I wasn't spooked. The Story didn't get me. I thanked them. I didn't cry.

Doreen stops, forkful almost at her mouth. How come?

Don't be making a documentary, Doreen. I talked to one of those today already.

I forgot about that. You put up your customary caution flags to Mr. Dutchman, I assume?

I said what I feel if that's what you mean.

And he was—

He was okay with it. It doesn't mean he'll call me or I'll call him. I don't know the etiquette. There's plenty of Toms.

I'm not so sure about that, dodo.

He told me he hated the war.

A man after my own heart. I wonder how many people he'll confide that to.

It doesn't matter. He's going to do what he's going to do. Aim cameras and microphones.

No one's getting executed, Tom. Ease up. Eat some more curry. You don't have to be living history every moment.

We'll talk with them too—who loses and who wins; who's in and who's out—

You think I'm always too hard, don't you? But I'm not always. There is no always. I'm a slow learner but I'm getting that. Forever tells lies like everyone else.

A whistling sound comes out of me: *Hooo! Hooo!*

I don't know, Tom, you may be bigger than the hole in you. How's that for optimism? With that, Doreen comes over to my side of her Formica dinette table. Sometimes—and she affixes an index finger to my forehead—I flat out love you. Don't say anything. Please. Let a girl be entitled to her mistakes.

I'll speak a prophecy ere I go.

It's around dawn when I get to the Wall. Doreen lent me her car. I like the feel of how empty the streets are. Some of the guys who came back from the war moved to the hinterlands: no more people anywhere near them, had it with people. Something bad is bound to happen with people, better the coyotes than people.

Are you numb, sir? Are you weary? Has grief absorbed your very pulse?

The sun's barely up but a few souls are already there. They look like mannequins—frozen in poses, one with his arm against the Wall as if holding it up, one crouched before it, one standing parade-ground straight a few feet away. These are all men but there's a woman, too. She's walking slowly along the length of the memorial, clutching her sweater close to her. It's cold this November morning. She's murmuring what I guess is a name over and over. Two syllables.

What do I want? If I say *nothing*, that bottomless word, then I'm avoiding, trying to be cool, above it all. That's not Tom. Tom is embroiled. Tom is stuck—lurching around but stuck. Nothing cool about Tom.

It's come to this is what I think, this big slab of stone. All the moments, the jokes and screaming and waiting and crossing the days off the calendar and the moments where death becomes you, have solidified into this. The spare November light begins to hit the stone and it's beautiful, the dark glow. It couldn't help but be beautiful and that's more heartrending, of course, the sentiment as far as away from what happened as could be.

The solidity consoles me, mortifies me, scares me, saddens me. The silence feels right, though. This is what too much looks like. I get that, not some statue of some soldiers—that holy crap of every war—but this mass, implacable and graven. The Wall has got death right.

I walk awhile, stop now and then, but I don't read. Maybe my motion is a form of praying. Or meditating. I did a little of that once. The sunlight is more pronounced.

Come and touch our doom, come and touch it.

An older man has shown up. His white hair is on the long side, wild, like he hasn't used a comb lately. He's got on some kind of topcoat. He walks over to me.

> A depth of sorrow I'd not believed
> Before I came to stand here and watch the sun
> Soften these un-lost names.
> I wish to speak each one, a memory of the tongue.

You see me?
I do.
You hail from?
Near Boston.
And you were—
There.

153

A dreadful teacher no doubt
Though who among us knows the worst? In eagerness
We seek to speak to it. My dead son's words are vanished.
No comparing. No company.
Do you hear me?
I do.

I had to come here, not to resolve my agony
Which is no longer agony but an ache in me,
My dullness depending toward my own death,
Absence stubbornly importuning.

And you?
I wanted to see it so I could leave it.
You speak for me and to me. Your name is?
Tom.
Well, Tom, I'll linger a bit and then I'll have this in me, whatever that means, and I'll tell my son tonight what I did. He won't say anything. I'm not that much of a crazy.
I am scarce in breath.
As am I, Tom. As am I.

ACKNOWLEDGEMENTS

Thanks to the early readers for their encouragement: Michael Steinberg, Peter Agrafiotis, Diana Goetsch, Jay Franzel, Jim Provencher, David Cappella, Eleanor Garron, Doug Rawlings, Owen Wormser and Sherry Rhynard. Thanks to all the people at New Rivers Press who helped make this book. Special thanks to Alan Davis for his belief in this book, the multi-talented Eugenia Kim for her wise counsel, Jennifer Rider for strategic thinking, and my wife Janet for more than I can ever enumerate.

NEW RIVERS PRESS emerged from a drafty Massachusetts barn in winter 1968. Intent on publishing work by new and emerging poets, founder C. W. "Bill" Truesdale labored for weeks over an old Chandler & Price letterpress to publish three hundred fifty copies of Margaret Randall's collection, *So Many Rooms Has a House But One Roof.*

Nearly four hundred titles later, New Rivers, a non-profit and now teaching press based since 2001 at Minnesota State University Moorhead, has remained true to Bill's goal of publishing the best new literature—poetry and prose—from new, emerging, and established writers.

New Rivers Press authors range in age from twenty to eighty-nine. They include a silversmith, a carpenter, a geneticist, a monk, a tree-trimmer, and a rock musician. They hail from cities such as Christchurch, Honolulu, New Orleans, New York City, Northfield (Minnesota), and Prague.

Charles Baxter, one of the first authors with New Rivers, calls the press "the hidden backbone of the American literary tradition." Continuing this tradition, in 1981 New Rivers began to sponsor the Minnesota Voices Project (now called Many Voices Project) competition. It is one of the oldest literary competitions in the United States, bringing recognition and attention to emerging writers. Other New Rivers publications include the American Fiction Series, the American Poetry Series, New Rivers Abroad, and the Electronic Book Series.